Josie couldn't ... with Adam aga...

She turned around in bed to kiss him…and saw a stranger staring back at her! Josie screamed in shock, scrambling out of the bed and dragging the black satin sheet with her.

The man arched a dark brow as he sat up on one elbow. "Is something wrong?"

This couldn't be happening to her. The naked man before her was *not* Adam Delaney. Her boyfriend had blond hair and blue eyes. This stranger had thick brown hair and keen brown eyes that seemed to penetrate the sheet in front of her. She sucked in a deep breath. "There's been a horrible mistake."

He blinked at her words and reached for his navy blue boxer shorts. "It's a little late for regrets now, isn't it?"

He couldn't begin to know how much she regretted last night. When she'd stolen in to her boyfriend's dark bedroom, she certainly hadn't expected there to be another man in it! "Who are you?"

"Don't you remember calling out my name last night?" He met her gaze. "I am Adam Delaney."

Dear Reader,

A dark night. Satin sheets. Sexy lingerie. All the necessary ingredients for an incredible night of passion. Only, Josie Sinclair's perfect seduction plan doesn't include finding a stranger in her boyfriend's bed! A man who won't let her forget how perfect they are together.

Josie's a "play-it-safe" librarian who does anything to avoid getting burned. Adam's a "live-for-adventure" photographer who's always playing with fire. Neither one of them expects the chemistry between them to flare so quickly out of control…

I hope you like this latest instalment of the fabulous WRONG BED mini-series. As an author, I love the concept of bringing two such different people as Adam and Josie together in such a unique way. Please drop me a line and let me know what you think of their story. You can reach me through my website at www.KristinGabriel.com or write to PO Box 5162, Grand Island, NE 68802-5162, USA.

All my best,

Kristin Gabriel

Look for a new Sensual Romance from Kristin Gabriel in the summer – *Night After Night*…
It will be another THE WRONG BED story.

STRANGERS IN THE NIGHT

by

Kristin Gabriel

MILLS & BOON®

For Bruce—my own "live-for-adventure" guy.

*MILLS & BOON and MILLS & BOON with the Rose Device
are registered trademarks of the publisher.*

*First published in Great Britain 2005
by Harlequin Mills & Boon Limited,
Eton House, 18-24 Paradise Road, Richmond, Surrey TW9 1SR*

© Kristin Eckhardt 2004

ISBN 0 263 84411 0

21-0405

*Printed and bound in Spain
by Litografia Rosés S.A., Barcelona*

1

JOSIE SINCLAIR HELD HER BREATH as she opened the apartment door, wincing at the slight squeal of the hinges. After slipping inside, she didn't breathe again until she'd closed the door behind her, locking it once more. Then she pocketed the key, debating the risk of switching on a light. She didn't want to do anything that might alert Adam to her presence.

Not until she was ready for him.

A full moon shone through the high-rise window, illuminating a shadowy path into the living room. A sudden hiss permeated the deep silence and Josie's hand flew to her chest. But it was only Horatio, her boyfriend's temperamental Siamese. She bent down to pet the cat, her heart still racing in her chest. Her reaction had more to do with nerves than fear. She'd never done anything like this before.

Horatio seemed to sense her anxiety, jerking away from her and bounding underneath the sofa. As she rose to her feet, Josie reached into her bag and pulled out the list she'd made on the flight from Tempe. Lists always made her feel in control and she began to calm

down as she found a pen in her bag to check off the
first item.

1. *Go to Adam's apartment.*

He'd given her a key weeks ago, but she hadn't
worked up the nerve to use it until tonight. Doubts
had assailed her on the long drive from the Denver
airport, but she'd stuck one of her motivational tapes
into the car's cassette player and now she was ready
for action. Almost. Her gaze moved to the second item
on the list.

2. *Undress.*

With trembling fingers, she untied the silk scarf
around her neck, then dropped it into the small bag
she'd brought with her from the airport. The fluttering
fabric enticed Horatio, who leaped out from under the
sofa and pounced on it immediately, batting at the
scarf with his paws.

She tried to take the scarf away from him, but his
claws snagged the delicate fabric and she knew it was
a lost cause. Ignoring the cat and his new toy, Josie
kicked off her shoes before shedding her slacks and
blouse. She tucked them all neatly into the bag, then
pulled out a sheer red negligee, holding it up in front
of her.

The transparent fabric and baby-doll design left little to the imagination, but the saleswoman at the bou-
tique in Tempe had assured her that any man would
find it irresistible.

Maybe she shouldn't wear anything at all.

Josie discarded that idea almost as soon as it entered her head. She wasn't *that* motivated. Her body was far from perfect, with her average bust and full hips. That was one of the reasons she wanted to surprise Adam in the dark. The negligee wouldn't provide much cover, but it was definitely better than nothing.

After slipping off her cotton bra, she dropped the negligee over her head. The hem whispered against the top of her thighs and a shiver rippled over her bare skin. Feeling overexposed, Josie took a deep breath and picked up the pen, slashing a line through the second item.

She had left Denver a week ago, after Adam had told her he wanted to take their relationship to the next level. She'd needed time to think about it, to debate all the pros and cons in her head before making a final decision. Josie had learned the hard way that acting strictly on emotion usually led to disaster.

Now bored with the scarf, Horatio leaped into a chair to watch her as she glanced at Item Three on her list.

3. Perfume.

The tiny but expensive perfume bottle she'd purchased in Tempe lay at the bottom of the bag, padded with several layers of bubble wrap to keep it from breaking. According to her research, this particular perfume was the most popular brand on the market. Josie dabbed the fragrance behind her ears, then touched her pulse points as the subtle aroma of jasmine filled the air.

The cat sneezed once, then jumped off the chair and disappeared into the kitchen. She just hoped the perfume didn't have the same effect on Adam.

They'd been dating for three months, which was almost a record for her. Most men didn't stick around for more than one date, once she made it clear that she wouldn't be hopping into bed with them anytime soon. Passion too often made people irrational and she wasn't about to let herself fall into that trap. A trap that had destroyed her family.

She mentally shook herself, not allowing the past to interfere with the present. Her decision to sleep with Adam was based on logic as well as emotion. She liked him and he seemed to possess the qualities she was looking for in a man. Stability, common sense and a good work ethic. If it turned out they were physically compatible, she could start thinking about a future with him.

But first things first. After checking off Item Three, her gaze moved down the list to Item Four.

4. Protection.

No doubt Adam had his own supply of condoms, but she wasn't about to take any chances. She'd stopped at a drugstore just outside the airport and had spent twenty minutes comparing the different brands before finally making her purchase.

Retrieving the shopping bag from the side compartment of her bag, she hesitated, wondering if carrying the entire box of two dozen condoms into his bedroom might be too intimidating. She took out one and tucked the flat foil package into the waistband of her new red-lace panties, then dropped the box back into the bag.

Only one item remained. She took a deep breath, quickly scanning the list to see if there was something else she might have forgotten. Now that the moment was at hand, more doubts began to assail her. What if Adam didn't like surprises? What if he wasn't in a romantic mood? What if she didn't please him? Or he didn't please her?

There were so many variables that she couldn't control. But her only alternative was to walk away and she'd done that too often in the past. At twenty-seven, she was ready for something more in her life than her career. She'd worked hard to put herself through college, graduating with honors before going on to earn her Master's degree in Library Science. Now she intended to put that same focused effort into her personal life.

Squaring her shoulders, she moved toward the bedroom, her bare feet padding silently on the thick carpet. When she opened the bedroom door, soft moonlight spilled from the living room into the darkness beyond, allowing her to just barely make out the shape of her boyfriend beneath the covers in the double bed.

Her mouth dry, Josie closed the door behind her, though her hand still gripped the brass knob. A deep, velvety darkness enveloped the room, calming her a little. She released the door knob, then moved blindly in the direction of the bed, led by the sound of Adam's soft, somnolent breathing.

When her toes bumped into the footboard, Josie knew she'd reached her destination. A small groan of pain escaped her, followed by the sound of Adam stirring on the bed. She froze, hoping she was as invisible to him in the darkness as he was to her.

Because something told her that if he awoke and switched on the light before she was ready, she'd never go through with the last and most important item on her list.

5. *Seduce Adam.*

ADAM DELANEY DREAMED of India, the scent of jasmine drifting in the summer air as his raft bobbed along the Alaknanda River. The majestic Himalayas stretched toward the cobalt-blue sky as he floated down the river, a woman's soft breath caressing his cheek.

The raft bobbed again and awareness invaded his sleep, arousing him enough to realize he wasn't lying on a river raft, but in his own bed. The mattress dipped with the weight of a body moving beside him. Even as full consciousness nagged at him, he kept his eyes closed, wanting to lose himself in the dream.

It had been too long since he'd been to India. The kaleidoscope of people and cultures and scenery always enticed him back. Just like his dream girl was enticing him now, touching his body with the barest of caresses.

Only it wasn't a dream.

Adam opened his eyes as slender fingers trailed over his shoulder and down the length of his arm. Total darkness blanketed the room. He turned over to face the woman beside him, the bedsprings creaking as her scantily clad body rolled against his own. She gasped at the contact and his groin instantly tightened at the feel of her lush curves and the creamy smoothness of her skin.

He heard an audible swallow, then she whispered, ''Surprise, Adam.''

It was a hell of a surprise—in more ways than one. *Who was she?* He didn't recall bringing a woman home with him last night. Adam had met several women at the bar earlier that evening, but he couldn't remember all of their names. In truth, he couldn't remember much of anything. Just another sign that he'd been drinking too much lately.

But he was completely sober now, his mind and his body both fully awake. He opened his mouth to ask the woman her name when she suddenly kissed him full on the lips, catapulting her body on top of him. Her breasts pressed against his chest with nothing but a thin layer of silky fabric between them. He groaned at the sensation, the feel of skin and silk against his hard frame chasing everything else from his mind.

Her kiss tasted sweet and innocent and slightly desperate, her mouth moving awkwardly over his lips. He gently cupped her cheeks with his hands, his thumbs lightly brushing the corners of her mouth until she finally relaxed against him, her body settling into his. Then he deepened the kiss, his tongue venturing into the satin depths of her mouth.

At that moment, Adam knew he'd never kissed this woman before. If he had, he'd damn well remember her name. But desire trumped curiosity, leading Adam to act now and ask questions later. Deprived of the sense of sight, his other senses kicked into high gear. He touched her. Tasted her. Inhaled her unique scent, a blend of sweet jasmine and willing woman that he found even more intoxicating than alcohol.

He gently rolled her onto her back, still kissing her as he took his time exploring uncharted territory. His tongue stroked over and around hers, while his hands mapped out the lush terrain of her body. His fingers gently traversed the slope of her breasts to their taut peaks. He lingered there awhile, caressing her nipples though the thin fabric of the negligee until low, hungry moans sounded deep in her throat.

Her arms tightened around his neck as she rolled onto her side, still kissing him as her fingers pressed into his unshaven jaw. Then her hands moved lower, tentatively exploring the breadth of his chest. Her fingertips danced across his skin, their featherlight touch driving him crazy. They moved even lower, skimming his ribs and belly and teasing the elastic waistband of his boxer shorts, but never quite reaching the part of him that he wanted her to touch the most.

Aching for her, Adam curved his hands over her lush, round bottom. Then he squeezed her tightly against him, relishing the friction of her against his heavy groin. He didn't even know her name, but at this moment he wanted her more than he could ever remember wanting any woman. He *needed* her. Now. Right now.

His hands slipped beneath her negligee to tangle with her panties, his body throbbing with urgency. He ripped them away, the delicate lace tearing with little effort on his part.

"Wait, I..." she gasped, fumbling for her torn panties on the mattress.

A groan bubbled in his throat and he prayed that she hadn't changed her mind. Or worse, that this really was a dream and she'd suddenly vanish into the mist. Instead, she pressed something into his palm.

"I brought this," she whispered.

He breathed a sigh of relief, feeling the familiar shape of the foil package. He smiled into the darkness. His dream girl had come prepared.

Adam shed his boxer shorts, then sat up on the edge of the bed. As he ripped the package open, he felt her body tense behind him. A moment later, he turned back to her, pressing tender kisses against her mouth and throat. She breathed a soft sigh against his ear, relaxing now as his lips moved lower. She moaned, leaning back against the feather pillows, her fingers threading through his hair.

His lips slid over her collarbone to the bodice of the negligee, where his tongue teased her nipple through the sheer fabric. When the tiny peak pebbled beneath his tongue, he lifted his head just far enough to pull the negligee off of her, then he bent down to tenderly suck the other nipple into his mouth.

"Please," she implored, her body arching under him.

"Hmm," he murmured under his breath, sharing her need but taking his time anyway, savoring this feast of the senses. Her wanton pleas in his ears. Her skin hot and dewy against his hands. The scent of jasmine in his nostrils. The unique taste of her heated kisses. Now what he wanted most was to see her when she came apart in his arms.

Adam shifted to turn on the bedside lamp, but she rolled on top of him before he got the chance. She straddled his hips with her thighs, her hair brushing his chest as she bent down to kiss him. First his mouth, then his chin, then she flicked her tongue over one flat nipple. She shackled his wrists with her hands, raising his arms above his head.

Adam forced himself to relinquish all control, letting her set the pace. Hell, he'd let her do anything as long as she didn't stop touching him. He didn't know if it was making love to an anonymous woman in the dark, or the woman herself, but he was on fire for her.

She drove him to the brink with her hands and her mouth, inflaming every inch of him until Adam couldn't take it anymore. He grasped her hips, positioning her above him, then thrust into her with one long, hard stroke. A low grunt of satisfaction ripped from his chest.

"Yes," she breathed on a whispered sigh, taking him deeper.

He closed his eyes, almost dizzy with wanting her. He couldn't remember her name or the last time he'd felt this way—if he'd ever felt this way. Then he couldn't remember his *own* name when she began to move on him.

His dream girl morphed into a wild woman, now rocking against him with an abandon that shattered his control. He matched her primitive rhythm, stroke for delicious stroke, both of them hurtling toward the precipice, helpless to stop or even slow down.

"Adam," she gasped, grabbing on to his shoulders, her fingers digging into his flesh.

She was so close. He braced her hips with his hands, pressing himself even deeper inside of her. The movement made her breath catch in her throat. Then her head lolled back and she shouted his name into the night. He followed her, free-falling into the abyss with a hoarse cry of satisfaction.

When he came to himself again, he found her cuddled against his chest. Adam wrapped his arms around her, neither one of them saying a word. In that moment, he felt as if their souls were as connected as their bodies.

A ridiculous reaction, since he didn't even remember her name. No doubt he'd come to his senses in the morning, he thought, his eyelids drifting shut.

But for now, he'd just enjoy the dream.

JOSIE WOKE UP SMILING.

She lay wrapped in Adam's arms, her back pressing against his chest and his chin resting on top of her head. Muted sunlight shone through the bedroom drapes, casting golden shadows over the bed as morning dawned in Denver. Her smile widened as she burrowed even closer against his warm, naked body. Last night had been more wonderful than she'd ever imagined. Adam was the perfect lover. Tender. Giving. Sensational.

A blush warmed her all the way down to her toes when she thought of all the things he'd done to her. He'd taken the time to arouse her in ways she hadn't thought possible. Then Josie remembered everything *she'd* done to him and her blush deepened. She'd never acted that way with a man before. Never let herself go like that. But at least she had her answer—they were definitely compatible.

Their night together made her feel closer to Adam than ever before. Close enough to tell him everything about her life. To share her most painful secret. But how did she find the right words?

I sent my father to prison.

The last thing she wanted to do was bring her past into their relationship. But Adam deserved to know the truth. How her mother had left her husband for another man, taking twelve-year-old Josie with her. How her father, Glenn Sinclair, had snapped at the double loss and done something extreme. Something Josie still didn't completely understand.

Glenn had picked up his daughter for a weekend visit shortly after the bitter divorce, asking her to go with him on a grand adventure. She'd agreed, ready to do anything to see her father smile again. Not realizing her mother would be frantic when she didn't return at the designated time. Not knowing a little girl couldn't fix a broken heart.

They'd spent the next month and a half traveling from state to state, never staying in one place for long. Her father had continued to call their life on the road a grand adventure, but Josie had missed her mother— something she couldn't tell her father without making him cry.

Josie had come to believe her father needed her more than her mother did, but she couldn't help calling home late one night, just to hear her mother's voice again, and to assure her mother that she was all right.

The authorities had traced the call and tracked them down in Missouri. They were transported back to Colorado, where, to her horror, her father was sentenced to one year in prison on child abduction charges. Their grand adventure had turned into a grand disaster.

Josie closed her eyes and swallowed a sigh, knowing she couldn't keep evading her boyfriend's questions about her family. The sooner she told him the truth, the sooner they could move on with their own lives. Last night had shown her they were meant to be together. That she could trust him.

Adam stirred behind her and Josie felt a funny little quiver deep in her belly at the thought of making love to him again. She couldn't wait. Judging by the growing arousal pressed against her backside, neither could he.

She turned around to kiss him...and saw a stranger staring back at her!

Josie screamed in horror, scrambling out of the bed and dragging the black satin sheet with her. She clutched it to her chest, her heart pounding like a jackhammer. "Who are you?"

The man arched a dark brow as he sat up on one elbow. "I was about to ask you the same question."

He didn't seem to mind the fact that he was completely naked. Powerful muscles flexed in his broad shoulders and she couldn't help but notice the deep tan lines at his waist and thighs, not to mention his impressive erection. She jerked her gaze up again, heat flooding her face.

This couldn't be happening to her. She'd planned everything so carefully—taken every precaution. But something had gone terribly wrong. This man was *not* Adam. Her boyfriend had blond hair and light-blue eyes. This stranger was dark everywhere, with thick brown hair and keen brown eyes that seemed to penetrate the sheet in front of her.

Tender areas of her body reminded her just what this man had done to her last night—what they'd done *together*. She met his gaze and knew he was thinking the same thing. She gulped hard and retreated farther from the bed, until her back hit the wall.

"Is something wrong?" he asked, concern and confusion furrowing his brow.

She sucked in a deep breath. "There's been a horrible mistake."

He blinked at her words, then sat up and turned his back to her before she could read his expression. Leaning down to snatch his navy-blue boxer shorts off the floor, he said, "It's a little late for regrets now, isn't it?"

Regrets? He couldn't begin to know how much she regretted what happened between them last night. How would she ever explain it to her boyfriend? He'd never believe her. Especially when the two men were so physically different.

It had been too dark to see those differences last night, though she should have been able to feel some of them. The wide breadth of his chest and shoulders. The taut ripples of muscle across his belly. But in her own defense, she'd never seen her boyfriend without his clothes on before and she certainly hadn't expected to find another man in his bed!

Which brought up another question. *Where was her boyfriend?* "Do you mind telling me what you're doing here?"

He looked at her like she was crazy. "I live here."

"Adam Delaney lives here," she countered, wrapping the sheet around her. Josie recognized the heavy oak bedroom furniture and the African art on the walls and the colorful Persian rug on the beige carpet. Everything was familiar—except him.

"I *am* Adam Delaney." He met her gaze. "Don't you remember calling out my name last night?"

She was in no mood to reminisce. "You are *not* Adam. Not my Adam, anyway. I think I know my own boyfriend."

He frowned as he pulled on his boxer shorts, then rose to his feet. The man had a good three inches on her boyfriend and at least thirty pounds. How could she have let this happen? Adam would never believe her. Not in a million years.

"Look, lady," he said, "I don't know what your problem is, but I am Adam Delaney. This is my apartment. My bed."

"That's impossible."

"Do I have to show you my identification?" he asked, walking over to the dresser. He retrieved his wallet and pulled out his driver's license, along with his passport.

His name was there in black and white. Along with

his other vital statistics. She stared at his picture, won-dering if she was in the midst of some crazy night-mare. Then she spun on her heel and escaped into the living room. Feeling a little dizzy, she plucked her slacks and blouse out of her bag.

He followed her. "Now tell me who you are and how you got into my apartment."

She tucked the sheet under her chin to cover herself and hastily pulled on her clothes. She had no intention of giving this stranger her name or any other infor-mation. He already knew her much too well.

"Something's not right," she said, more to herself than to him. "I know this apartment. I know Horatio. I know Adam Delaney—and you're not him."

"You can call my mother if you'd like," he said wryly, leaning against the doorway. "She'll tell you that's been my name since the day I was born thirty years ago. She'll also tell you that I've been on a photo shoot in South America for the past four months. I just got back yesterday."

He had to be lying. Had he done something to her Adam? Hurt him? She finished dressing, then let the satin sheet fall to the floor. Her blouse was buttoned wrong, but she was too upset to care.

He advanced on her. "I think we should start over."

Her gaze dropped to the sizable bulge in his boxer shorts. What exactly did he mean by start over? Josie didn't intend to stick around long enough to find out. Whirling, she scooped up her overnight bag with one hand and ran toward the apartment door.

''Hey, wait a minute,'' he called after her.

She heard heavy footsteps behind her and almost tripped over the cat. But she reached the front door before he did, slamming it behind her, then she raced for the elevator at the end of the long hallway.

Luckily, the elevator doors slid open as soon as she pressed the button. She stumbled inside, then turned around in time to see him step out of his doorway and into the empty hallway. He still wore his boxer shorts and a befuddled expression on his ruggedly handsome face.

But she was the one who was confused. He claimed to be Adam Delaney. *Her* Adam Delaney. It just didn't make sense.

She jabbed several buttons on the elevator panel, not caring where she ended up as long as he didn't follow her. She wanted to get as far away from this man as possible. To forget last night had ever happened.

But when their gazes locked in the moment before the elevator doors closed, she knew forgetting him wouldn't be easy. Not when his touch was still branded on her skin and their lovemaking was still burned into her memory.

So she'd just have to settle for never seeing him again.

2

ADAM STARED AT THE ELEVATOR doors long after they had closed. His dream girl was gone. Worse, he realized she must be crazy. He also realized he'd never met her before, at the bar last evening or anywhere else. He'd known that as soon as he'd seen her this morning.

In his business, Adam never forgot a face. Hers was unique, with wide-set green eyes and high, sculpted cheekbones. He wouldn't describe her as beautiful, though her full lips and the tilt of her nose added an interesting dimension to her face that sparked his interest as a photographer.

The way she'd seduced him last night sparked his interest as a man. He'd wanted to make love to her again this morning, but the gleam of fear he'd seen in her green eyes had held him back. Despite his taste for dangerous pursuits, Adam didn't chase unwilling women. Or crazy ones.

With a sigh of disappointment, he walked back into his apartment, a dull throb in his head from too many beers the night before. Horatio was waiting by the door, his tail flicking impatiently behind him.

"You should have warned me," he muttered, moving toward the kitchen. But even as he said the words, he couldn't regret what had happened between him and his mystery lady. She'd touched his soul as well as his body, something no other woman could claim. Something he hadn't thought possible.

He reached into the cupboard for the bag of cat food, then froze. The shelves were stocked full. Cans of soup and vegetables. Boxes of cereal and granola bars. Several bags of assorted pasta. His cupboards had been almost bare when he'd left home four months ago.

"What the hell is going on here?"

Horatio replied with a loud meow, pacing beside his empty cat bowl. Adam filled it, then placed the bag back into the cupboard as more questions filled his head. How had his dream girl gotten into his apartment last night? How did she know his cat's name? How did she know *his* name?

Ten minutes later, he was fully dressed and ready for some answers. He knocked on the door directly across from his apartment, hoping Mrs. Clanahan was an early riser. His elderly neighbor had offered to feed and care for Horatio while Adam was out of the country. Before he'd left for Rio, he'd stocked up on cat food and kitty litter, then given her a spare key to his apartment.

Maybe Mrs. Clanahan could explain how all that food had magically appeared in his kitchen cupboards. And how that strange woman had magically appeared in his bed.

But when the door opened, it wasn't Mrs. Clanahan who greeted him but a middle-aged man wearing a torn white T-shirt and a pair of baggy red shorts. An old game show rerun blared on the television behind him and the stench of rotting meat permeated the air.

"Yeah?" the man said, scowling up at him.

"I'm looking for Mrs. Clanahan."

"She don't live here no more."

"Since when?"

"Since she fell down and broke her hip about three months ago. Her daughter lives in Florida, so she carted her down there and sublet this apartment to me."

Mrs. Clanahan had often talked about how much she missed her daughter. Too bad she'd had to break her hip to spend time with her. He felt a moment's concern about the sweet old lady's injury, but he had another matter to deal with.

"And you are?"

"Clyde Buckley," he replied, growing impatient. He craned his head over his own shoulder trying to watch his television show.

"So tell me, Mr. Buckley, what arrangements did Mrs. Clanahan make about Horatio?"

Buckley scowled as he turned back around. "Who the hell is Horatio?"

Adam hitched his thumb behind him. "The cat in

the apartment across the hall. Mrs. Clanahan was supposed to feed him while…"

"Oh, yeah," Buckley interjected, "that was part of the sublet agreement. But the guy came back early. Lucky thing, cause I'm allergic to cats."

Apprehension skittered over Adam's spine. "What guy?"

"The guy who lives there," Buckley replied, scratching his belly. "Delaney. He picked up the key and even gave me twenty bucks for all my trouble."

Adam didn't want to believe the man, but Clyde Buckley seemed incapable of artifice. He seemed barely capable of walking upright. "Did you ask him for some kind of identification?"

"Why should I?" Buckley retorted. "He knew the name of the damn cat. Who are you anyway and why are you here asking all these questions?"

He clenched his jaw. "*I'm* Adam Delaney. You gave my key to the wrong man."

Buckley stuck out his jaw. "So where's your identification?"

For the second time that morning, Adam pulled out his wallet and flashed his driver's license and passport.

Clyde Buckley leaned in for a closer look. "Okay, so it says your name is Adam Delaney. But you sure don't look much like him."

It wasn't even eight o'clock yet and Adam wanted a

drink, but his pounding head nixed that idea. "I think you mean he doesn't look much like me."

"Huh?"

Adam took a deep breath, trying not to lose his temper. It wasn't Buckley's fault that some jerk was trying to screw up his life. "Tell me what he looks like."

His gaze drifted to the television set. "Who?"

"Delaney."

Buckley looked back at him. "I thought you said you're Delaney."

"I am," he snapped. "I mean the man who told you he was me."

"Oh." Buckley crinkled his brow. "I can't really remember—I only saw him once or twice."

"Try."

The older man shrugged. "Maybe about six feet. Skinny. Needed a haircut."

"What else?" Adam asked, wanting specific details. "How about the color of his hair? His eyes? The kind of car he drives? Anything at all you can tell me."

Buckley snorted. "Hell, I don't know. I mind my own business around here, you know?"

"Did you ever see him with a woman?"

"Like I said, I mind my own business." Buckley paused for a moment. "There was a broad who showed up at his door once in a while, but don't ask me to describe her, 'cause she sure wasn't worth remembering."

Then it couldn't be his dream girl. Adam mentally

kicked himself for letting her go. He'd never find her again in a city of over two million people. She might be the only one who could answer all of his questions.

"I gotta go," Buckley said. "They're about to spin the big wheel."

The door closed in his face before Adam could say another word. He stared at it a moment, tempted to kick it down in frustration. But that wouldn't accomplish anything except alienating his new neighbor.

He turned around and walked back inside his apartment.

Adam couldn't deny it any longer. Someone had been impersonating him. But who? And for what reason? To find the answers, he began a thorough search of the apartment, hoping to find some clue to the man's real identity. He started with the bedroom, but the only thing he found that didn't belong to him was a lone black sock underneath the drapes.

When he walked into the living room, his gaze fell on the bookshelf. Two books caught his eye. He walked over and pulled them out, noting a sticker on each spine from the Denver Public Library. Books he hadn't checked out.

"*Success at Any Price,*" he muttered, reading one title. Then he looked at the other book. "*How to Change Your Life Forever.*"

His darkroom yielded more evidence. It had been a small bedroom that he'd converted into a darkroom to allow him to develop pictures at home. Several items had been moved and one of his old cameras was missing.

He continued his search, even digging though the trash cans in the bathroom and kitchen. It was clear from the amount of garbage he found that someone had been living here recently. Someone pretending to be him.

Adam strode into his office and opened his file cabinet. All his files were neatly in place, but that didn't mean the impostor hadn't combed through his records. They detailed almost everything about his life. Bank accounts and insurance policies. His professional contacts. Even all the names, addresses and telephone numbers of his family and friends in his hometown, Pleasant Valley, Colorado.

Adam had to figure out what the impostor had done with this information. But first, he needed to contact Cole Rafferty, a good friend and local private investigator, to find out just how badly this guy had screwed up his life. Then he'd call his editor at *Adventurer* magazine and tell him the trip to New Zealand would have to be delayed for a while. Because he wasn't going anywhere until his life was *his* again.

ON MONDAY MORNING, Josie rushed into the main branch of the Denver Public Library just before the doors opened to the public. Always punctual and professional, she drew stares from the other employees as she hurried to her desk. No doubt they'd all go into a state of shock if they were to discover Josephine Sinclair had spent Saturday night in the arms of a stranger.

A fact she didn't plan to divulge to anyone.

But she couldn't put it behind her, either. She'd spent most of last night tossing and turning in bed, then slept through her alarm this morning. Running late for work had only made her feel more harried, more out of control.

If only she'd never gone through with that surprise midnight seduction. But Josie so often resisted the urge to do something wild and spontaneous that she'd been unable to help herself.

With disastrous results.

After settling in behind her desk, she straightened her nameplate and the electric pencil sharpener, then untangled the telephone cord. She had to put her life in order again. But to do that she needed some answers.

As a reference librarian, she excelled at providing information to patrons on some of the most bizarre subjects imaginable. Now she was the one in need of information. Cold, hard facts about Adam Delaney that would tell her why she'd found a stranger in her boyfriend's bed.

By late morning, she'd discovered enough to start a folder. Inside, she placed back issues of *Adventurer* magazine that featured his photographs and added printouts of newspaper articles she'd found on the Web site of his hometown, Pleasant Valley, Colorado.

What she hadn't found was a picture of him.

Frustrated, Josie sorted through the *Pleasant Valley Gazette*'s articles once again. A weekly paper, it focused on local news in the small town, and she'd found several feature stories in it about the hometown hero's adventures, including Adam's harrowing rescue of a Siamese cat in Egypt.

According to the article, Adam had been raised on an acreage just outside of Pleasant Valley and had always had an affinity for animals. So he'd brought the cat back to Denver with him. Josie already knew all of this—Adam had told her the story himself, modestly downplaying his heroic role in saving Horatio.

But he'd never told her anything about the man she'd found in his bed on Saturday night. Despite her extensive search, she still didn't know why he was there or what he'd done with Adam. *Her* Adam.

She'd tried e-mailing her boyfriend, as well as calling him on his cell phone all day yesterday. But for some reason he wasn't answering.

Or he wasn't able to answer.

She suppressed a shiver, not wanting to believe the worst. Her boyfriend was safe—he had to be. She couldn't make love to a man capable of violence, could she? Not only make love to him, but thoroughly enjoy it. She groaned under her breath, then buried her face in her hands.

Josie had never before indulged in one-night stands or anonymous sex. She preferred to play it safe in both her professional and personal life. Despite the erotic allure, sleeping with a stranger was a risk she'd simply never been willing to take.

But no matter how hard she tried to forget, the night she'd spent in her stranger's arms kept flashing into her mind. The way he'd touched and kissed and tantalized her until she'd become someone she didn't recognize. Wild and wanton and begging him for sweet release. Heat suffused her cheeks as she closed the file, wondering how she could have acted that way. And how she would ever explain what had happened between them to her boyfriend.

But she had to find him first.

Then Josie looked up and saw the stranger she wanted to forget, the one who claimed *he* was Adam Delaney, walk through the door.

She grabbed a magazine, almost ripping it in half as she held it open in front of her face, hoping he hadn't seen her. But her hopes died when she heard footsteps approaching her desk.

"Excuse me." His familiar, whiskey-smooth voice sent ripples over her skin.

"Yes?" she said behind the magazine. Too late, she realized it was a copy of *his* magazine. Her gaze moved from a spectacular aerial photograph of the Grand Canyon to a small blurb at the bottom of the page that credited Adam Delaney as the photographer who had taken the picture while skydiving.

"I'm hoping you can help me."

She slowly lowered the magazine until just her eyes peeked over the top of it. "What do you need?"

He placed two books on the desk. "These were left in my apartment and I need to know who checked them out."

"Perhaps someone at the front desk can help you," she replied, relieved that he didn't recognize her. Of course, the last time he'd seen her she'd been wearing a sheet. Today she wore a light-gray suit and her blond hair pulled back into a neat French braid.

He hesitated, his gaze narrowing. "Have we met?"

She looked up at him, the magazine still concealing half her face. "I don't think so."

He stared into her eyes. "You're her. You're my dream girl."

"Hardly," she said, lowering the magazine and facing the man she'd never wanted to see again. "I'm sorry, but you'll have to ask someone else for assistance."

But he didn't take the hint. Instead, he pulled her pink scarf out of his shirt pocket. "Don't you remember leaving this at my place?"

Mortified, Josie reached out and snatched it from him, all too aware of the stares from some of the staff. "Please lower your voice. This is not the time or the place to cause a scene."

A wry smile curled up one corner of his mouth. "You call this a scene? I just want to talk to you."

"Not here," she insisted.

"Then where? I'm free all day," he said.

"I'd rather not talk about it at all," she told him. "We both know it was a huge mistake. So let's just forget it ever happened."

"Not an option." He leaned forward, planting both hands on her desk, a flash of fire in his brown eyes. "Some guy walked into my life and pretended he was me. Now I want to know why and, like it or not, you're my only connection to him."

He was so close she could see flecks of gold in his brown eyes and the tiny scar near the corner of his mouth. The same mouth that had tasted her lips. Her breasts. The tender skin inside her thighs. For a moment, Josie found it hard to breathe. "The Adam Delaney that I know would never do anything like that."

"Prove it."

She stood up, ready to do battle. This man seemed to bring out the passion in her—a reaction she didn't like one bit. "I don't have to prove anything to you!"

"Then I guess you leave me with no option but to go to the police."

"The police," she echoed, certain she'd heard him wrong.

He gave a slow nod. "I'd rather not, because they're going to want to know every detail about what happened between us. How you broke into my apartment in the middle of the night…''

"I had a key," she protested.

"How you took all your clothes off before climbing into my bed," he continued, as if she hadn't spoken. "How you even brought a condom with you…''

"All right," she cried, cutting him off, "I'll meet with you. Just tell me where and when."

He glanced at his watch. "It's almost noon. Why don't we meet for lunch at Spagli's on Bannock Street? That's not too far from here."

Josie had no appetite, but better to get it over with as soon as possible. "Fine. I'll see you there."

He smiled. "I'm looking forward to it."

Her fists clenched as she watched him leave. How dare he threaten to expose the most embarrassing moment of her life. She hated the fact that he had that kind of power over her—and hated even more that he seemed to enjoy it.

Josie had been tempted to go the police herself when he'd claimed he was Adam Delaney. The only thing that had stopped her was the very reason he'd cited. She'd be forced to tell them everything about the night she'd spent in his arms and she simply couldn't bring herself to do it.

Besides, she wanted to talk to Adam first. *Her Adam.* There had to be a reasonable explanation for this mess. Something she had yet to find in her research. She had yet to find her boyfriend, too, and that bothered her.

Josie sat back down at her desk, hating the way that her life was spinning out of control, just like it had when her father had been arrested. Only she'd been a child then, and now she was an adult. Perfectly capable of handling this or any other situation.

She took a deep breath, then another, aware of the quiet whispers of the staff at the front desk. How much had they overheard? Josie had never raised her voice at work before, even when dealing with the most irritating of library patrons. She had always prided herself on her self-control.

Now this man who called himself Adam Delaney had made her lose that control. Not once, but twice. The first time had been Saturday night, when she'd come completely undone in his arms. Then today, when he'd threatened to expose their illicit night together.

Josie didn't intend to let it happen again.

3

ADAM SAT AT A CORNER table in Spagli's, wondering which woman would show up—his dream girl or that hermetically sealed dragon at the library. He almost hadn't recognized her. She'd contained her wild side beneath a tidy hairstyle and a shapeless suit. Her attitude had undergone a radical change, too.

Which was fine with him. He didn't need to complicate this mess by lusting after his impostor's girlfriend. A woman by the name of Josephine Sinclair, according to the nameplate he'd seen on her desk.

Adam leaned back in his chair, oblivious to the diners around him. He'd never made love to a woman named Josephine before. Hell, he'd never met a woman like Josephine before, prickly on the outside, but peel off those layers and there was a warm and willing woman underneath.

Not that he intended to do any more peeling. At least not until he knew all the facts. It was entirely possible that Josephine was in on this scam. Maybe that night in his bed had been a setup. He'd volunteered enough hours at the legal-aid office in college to make him consider the situation from every angle.

Yet, he couldn't deny the horrified shock he'd seen on her face Sunday morning. Or the words she'd uttered that had hurt him more than he wanted to admit. *There's been a horrible mistake.*

Adam didn't believe in mistakes. His philosophy was that every day was an adventure and damn the consequences. Making love to Josephine Sinclair had been one of the most thrilling adventures he'd had in a very long time.

Too bad she didn't see it that way.

When she arrived at the restaurant, Adam reminded himself that she might not be as innocent as she appeared. He watched her walk toward the table, trying to assess her the same way he used to look over accused felons who came to legal aid looking for assistance. Most of them had been guilty of their crimes, but a few could pull off the innocent act.

Josephine Sinclair had it down pat. She walked briskly toward him with her head held high, a flush of indignation on her cheeks. She clutched a gray leather purse in her hand that matched her gray suit. He decided he liked her much better wearing nothing at all.

His gaze fell to the sway of her hips and those long legs beneath her gray skirt. The same legs that had wrapped around him Saturday night, flexing against his hips and thighs as she rode him. His groin tightened at the memory, making it somewhat uncomfortable for him to stand up to meet her.

"Right on time," he said, leaning over to pull out her chair.

"Let's just get this over with." She sat down, pushing away the menu in front of her.

Despite her impatience, Adam intended to take his time—just like he'd done Saturday night. "Shall we order a glass of wine first?"

She met his gaze, those beautiful green eyes filled with both intelligence and alarm. "Look, Mr....Delaney, I don't know what you want from me, but I don't consider this meeting a social occasion."

"Adam," he said evenly.

She blinked. "What?"

"I want you to call me Adam." He waved away an approaching waitress. "After all, we're hardly strangers. And I'll call you Jo."

"No, you won't," she countered. "Because after today you'll never see me again."

Her frostiness intrigued him, even though he knew it was an act. Why did Josie feel the need to hide behind her starchy Josephine persona? Who was she trying to fool?

"What did the impostor call you?" he asked.

"Who?" she said, then her eyes narrowed. "If you mean the real Adam, he called me Josie."

He leaned forward, the scent of jasmine teasing his nostrils. Or was he just imagining it? "I am the real Adam Delaney. So if you're not in on this scam to take over my life, then prove it."

"How can I possibly do that? If you really are Adam Delaney, then something is very wrong."

"Yes," he said bluntly. "Your so-called boyfriend's been deceiving you."

She lifted her chin. "That's a possibility I refuse to consider."

He wondered what kind of man would inspire this kind of loyalty in a woman. Didn't she know men lied all the time? He'd done it himself more times than he cared to remember, hoping to spare the woman's feelings when he was ready to move on.

Adam made it a habit to tell women up front that he wasn't looking for more than a good time, but somehow they never seemed to believe him. Each one thought she could be the woman to change his mind. To lead him down the aisle and confine him to a life of rules and responsibility. He'd given that up three years ago when he'd bypassed a chance to attend Yale Law School.

A decision he'd never regretted. Adam still remembered the fateful day when his college roommate had walked into their dorm room and told him about the photography contest sponsored by *Adventurer* magazine. Photography had always been just a hobby for him, though he'd been talented enough to earn a job on the college newspaper.

No one in the Delaney family, least of all Adam, had considered that he might make photography a career.

He was supposed to go to law school and eventually take over his father's practice in Pleasant Valley.

But winning that contest changed everything. Along with a cash prize from the magazine, he'd received a lucrative job offer as a staff photographer. It had taken him three days to decide which career path to take. The safe, boring world of law or the exciting and sometimes dangerous world of outdoor photography.

In the end, his yearning for adventure had won out over the security of a legal career.

His editor at *Adventurer* magazine loved him because he was willing to go anywhere and do anything in pursuit of the perfect shot. He had some great ones, but none that completely satisfied him. He was still searching for the defining photograph of his career. If shooting it meant hanging off the side of a mountain in Nepal or taking a raft down the Amazon River, then so be it.

Adam had never shied away from danger. Even the thought of pursuing his impostor gave him a rush of adrenaline. It didn't matter whether he was chasing lions on an African savanna or chasing human prey. He thrived off the challenge.

"Why did you insist on meeting with me today?" Josie asked, breaking his reverie. "I checked into those two books you brought into the library. They were taken out with a library card in Adam Delaney's name. So there's nothing more I can do to help you."

Can't or won't? He stared at her for a moment, wondering how she'd like life on a savanna. With her blond hair loose and blowing in the breeze. Her creamy skin turning a golden tan under the hot sun. Midnight swims in a freshwater pool. He swallowed a wistful sigh. Jo might like it, but Josephine would hate it.

"Well?" she asked, impatience lacing her tone. "Why am I here?"

He smiled, telling himself that annoying Josephine might be as dangerous as poking a lioness with a stick. "Maybe I just couldn't wait to see you again."

"This isn't a joke...Adam."

He noticed how hard it was for her to call him by that name and for a moment felt a twinge of guilt for teasing her. If she truly had been deceived by his impostor, then they should become allies, not enemies.

But first she had to earn his trust. "Tell me about your boyfriend."

She hesitated. "What exactly do you want to know?"

"Everything, but let's start with the basics first. How about giving me his physical description."

"Well, he looks nothing like you," she began, as if this was a good thing. "He's not quite as tall, not quite as big, not quite as..."

"Good in bed?" he ventured.

"I was going to say rude," she retorted, a deep

blush rising to her cheeks, "but I didn't want to offend you. Obviously, I shouldn't have worried about it."

He hadn't intended to embarrass her, but something about Josephine's austere manner provoked him. Adam found himself wanting to fluster her, hoping to see a hint of his wild woman beneath the cool exterior. The woman he'd been thinking about too much since Saturday night.

"Go on," he cajoled. "What else can you tell me about Mr. Perfect?"

"I never said he was perfect," she countered. "But he is very responsible and levelheaded."

"Boring, in other words."

She tipped up her chin. "On the contrary, my Adam is everything a woman could want in a man."

"Except for the fact that your boyfriend's been living under *my* name, in *my* apartment, with *my* cat for the last few months."

"We only have your word on that."

He shrugged his shoulders. "I've already offered to let you call my mother. What more can I do to prove to you that I'm telling the truth?"

"Tell me something about Adam Delaney," she challenged. "The real Adam Delaney. His past, his work, his life. Because I've done enough research on the man myself, I probably know his life better than you do."

He grinned, ready to prove her wrong. "I was born in Pleasant Valley, Colorado, population five thou-

sand and twelve. My parents are Lila and Steven Delaney. Mom's a cook at the high school and my father
practices law."

"All facts you could have found in public records.
How about something more specific?"

"Maybe you should have put my impostor through
this interrogation before you started dating him."

"Maybe you should tell me more personal details
about Adam Delaney." She arched a brow. "Or don't
you know any?"

Now he felt like the one getting poked with a stick.

"I broke my ankle playing in the state basketball
tournament my senior year, but we won anyway. I
earned my bachelor's degree in Criminal Justice at the
University of Colorado in Boulder and got accepted to
Yale Law School. But I decided to travel the world instead."

She didn't say anything, but the color faded from
her cheeks.

"I know you believe me," Adam said softly, "even
if you don't want to admit it."

She shook her head. "I'm not sure what to believe.
You could have looked all that up in the archives of
the *Pleasant Valley Gazette.*"

"So could my impostor," Adam replied, ready to
end this battle between them. "Look, the fact is this
guy duped both of us. Now I'm not going to sit back
and let him get away with it. I plan to track him down
and I want you to help me."

Her green eyes widened. "How can I possibly help you?"

"The way I figure it, my impostor has to be someone I know. Someone who knew I'd be out of the country for several months. Hell, he even knew my neighbor across the hall was taking care of Horatio. He finagled the damn apartment key from him."

"Then maybe you should ask your neighbor to help you."

He shook his head. "Tried that. It's a dead end. You're the only one who can help me, Jo."

"Josie," she said, correcting him. "And I really don't want to get involved."

"It's too late. You got involved the moment you climbed into my bed."

She stood up. "A moment I intend to forget. I suggest you do the same."

But he wasn't about to let her walk away from him again. "It's your choice. Either help me voluntarily or I'll be forced to find out the information in other ways. Like having intimate conversations with all of your coworkers. Your friends. Your family. Anyone who might have seen the two of you together."

Her nostrils flared. "To tell them what? That I was dating an impostor? That you and I..."

"I'll do whatever is necessary to find out who did this," he declared, hoping she wouldn't call his bluff.

Fury lit her green eyes. "So, basically, you're blackmailing me?"

He thought about it for a moment. "Yes."

She shot him a look of pure loathing. "You are despicable."

"But never boring."

Josie turned and marched out of the restaurant without another word. He followed her, much too aware of the luscious body that lay underneath that boring suit. Maybe that's why she wore it—to keep strange men, like him, at bay. No doubt she regretted the intimate night they'd spent together.

He, on the other hand, couldn't seem to stop thinking about it. And that surprised him, since Adam rarely reminisced about one-night stands. But for some reason, Josie was different. Which might explain his reaction to her. He'd always loved a challenge.

Adam caught up with her on the sidewalk. "I want your answer."

She kept walking. "Too bad. I'm due back at work."

"And I've got an assignment waiting for me halfway across the world. It might be an inconvenience to both of us, but I need to find this impostor so I can get on with my life. Will you help me?"

She whirled on him. "I can't help you. I don't have any idea where Adam is. I mean, my Adam."

For some reason, the way she kept saying *my Adam* grated on him. "We both need answers. That's why we should work together to find him."

She arched a skeptical eyebrow. "How do you suggest we do that?"

"Simple. I'll introduce you to everyone I know here in Denver. Like I said before, this impostor has to be someone who knows me—knows personal details about my life. When you spot your boyfriend, just point him out to me."

She hesitated, obviously mulling over his plan in her mind. "And then?"

"And then we never have to see each other again."

JOSIE STARED UP AT HIM, resisting the temptation to slide her palm over the shadow of whiskers on his jaw. He stood much too close to her, making it impossible to think clearly. But she refused to back away from him or give him any other signs of retreat. A man like Adam would use it to his advantage, and he already seemed to have all the advantages, which left her caught in a trap she couldn't escape.

A trap of her own making.

"Fine," she said at last, knowing she had little choice. Though she truly did want to find her boyfriend. To feel safe again. "The sooner we end this, the better."

He smiled. "Methinks you protest too much."

His smile made something warm uncurl in her belly. She ignored the sensation, telling herself it was a hunger pain. "In your dreams."

"My dreams have been quite stimulating lately."

She didn't know what he was talking about and told herself she didn't want to know. Adam was everything her boyfriend was not—brash, pushy and over-confident. She couldn't wait to prove him wrong.

So why not join him in his search and discover the truth? Maybe her boyfriend was in trouble. Maybe he needed her. She looked up at the man in front of her, wondering if he'd ever needed anyone.

"Well?" he said, waiting for her answer.

"All right, I'll help you."

"Good choice," he said with an approving nod. "We'll start tonight."

"Start what exactly?" she asked, hoping she hadn't just made a big mistake.

"The hunt."

She saw the gleam of anticipation in his dark eyes and wondered if this was only a game to him. Another adventure he could add to his extensive collection.

Josie had endured enough adventures growing up to last her a lifetime. Now she just wanted stability in her life. A good job. A place she could call home. A man who made her feel safe and secure. Like her boy-friend. The complete opposite of the man standing in front of her, who could stir up passionate emotions in-side of her that she hadn't known existed. Emotions that she didn't want to feel.

Passion had made her mother leave her father for another man. It had made her father steal her away out of desperation and revenge. Passion had de-stroyed her family. But she refused to let it rule her now. She had to control herself, no matter how much he provoked her.

"Let's meet at my apartment around seven," he suggested. "Unless you want me to pick you up at your place?"

"No," she blurted, uneasy at the prospect of him invading her home—and her life. She wanted to keep him at a distance, if that was possible, even if it meant returning to that apartment, the scene of the biggest mistake of her life. "I'll meet you there at seven."

Then she spun on her heel and stepped off the curb and into oncoming traffic. A car horn blasted and something jerked her off her feet.

A moment later, she found herself in Adam's arms. He held her on the sidewalk, her body clasped tightly against his own. "That was a close one."

It took her a moment to find her voice. He'd probably just saved her life. He'd also been the reason she'd stepped into traffic without looking. "I suppose I should thank you."

"Don't worry about it." Concern etched his brow. "It's probably my fault."

"Yes," she agreed, distracted by the soft touch of his fingers caressing her cheek. She wanted to close her eyes and enjoy the sensation. To let him soothe away the fear and uncertainty quaking inside of her.

His arms tightened around her and Josie could feel the hard length of his body aligned with her own. She shifted slightly, fitting more intimately against him before coming to her senses.

She pulled away from him. "I have to get back to work."

"Are you sure you're all right?" he asked, watching her smooth down her suit.

"Positive," she lied, then turned away from him and waited for the Walk light to appear. After checking the traffic in both directions, Josie headed across the street, sensing that Adam was still watching her.

As she walked to the library, Josie relived the experience over and over again. The oncoming car. Adam's rescue. Her temporary insanity in his arms. Just more proof that the man was dangerous.

By the time she reached her desk, her emotions were once again firmly in check. Until the head librarian, Evelyn Myerson, approached her.

"I have a phone message for you," Evelyn said, handing Josie a note.

Was it a message from Adam? Her Adam? She took the note from her, aware that Evelyn was still standing in front of her desk as she quickly scanned it. The message wasn't from her boyfriend, but from her mother.

Disappointment rushed through her as she read the note, questioning why Josie had missed joining her for Sunday dinner. The shock of waking up in bed with the wrong man had made her completely forget about her mother's dinner invitation.

"Thank you," Josie said, tucking the message inside her skirt pocket.

Evelyn took a step closer to the desk and lowered her voice. "You seem a bit distracted today. I hope everything is all right."

The head librarian had always given Josie stellar evaluations, impressed by her willingness to take on any task assigned to her. Evelyn Myerson didn't tolerate messy work habits or disorganization. A widow with no children, she'd made the library her life.

"I'm fine," Josie assured her.

Evelyn sighed. "You do excellent work, Josie, so I have no complaints in that department. However, I must ask that you handle any personal conflicts on your own time. If you need to take a few days off, I'm sure we can arrange it."

She clenched her jaw, surmising that Evelyn had witnessed her altercation with Adam this morning. Her boss was a stickler for adhering to library policy and rules, something Josie had always admired about her. But at this moment, she'd prefer it if Evelyn minded her own business.

"That won't be necessary," Josie said. "What happened this morning will never happen again."

"Good," Evelyn replied, then she looked at her watch. "You still have a few minutes left on your lunch break. If you'd like to take that time to return the phone call, I suggest you do so."

Josie rose from her desk, knowing she might risk

another lecture if her mother called back during working hours. What else could possibly go wrong today? It seemed her life had started falling apart the moment she'd climbed into Adam's bed. Maybe once she got him out of her life, everything would return to normal again.

After calling her mother to apologize for missing dinner, Josie walked out of the break room and back to her desk, trying to lose herself in her work. A task that proved impossible.

Tomorrow would be better, Josie told herself, as she wound her up shift. She just needed time to adjust to these new complications in her life. To deal with them in a logical and rational manner. She'd let emotions drive her today and that had been a mistake.

Starting tonight, she'd stay in complete control. No matter what Adam said or did, she wouldn't let him rattle her. Saturday night had been an aberration. A mistake that wouldn't happen again.

No matter how much he tempted her.

4

ADAM WASN'T CONVINCED his dream girl would show up until his doorbell rang at seven o'clock on the dot. He straightened his tie, surprised to find his heart give a lurch of anticipation as he walked to the door. Who would he find standing on the other side? Stiff-and-starchy Josephine or sweet-and-sexy Jo?

The contradiction between the two intrigued him. Challenged him. He found himself thinking more about her than about the man who had hijacked his life. What kind of woman had she been for her boy-friend? Had she ever climbed into that impostor's bed—which, come to think of it was Adam's own bed?

That unsettling question lingered in his mind as he answered the doorbell. She stood in the threshold, even more aloof than she'd been at lunch. The gray suit was gone, replaced by a navy-blue dress that reached below her knees. A dress fit for a funeral.

But her attempt to conceal her sexuality seemed to have the opposite effect on him. He found it oddly erotic and wondered what it would take to make her lose her cool composure. To rekindle the passion that had flamed so hot between them.

"May I come in?" she asked, making him realize he'd been staring at her for much too long.

"Of course," he said, opening the door wider. Horatio appeared behind him and the cat's tail flicked when he saw her. Horatio bounded up to her, rubbing his furry body against her ankles.

Adam watched her bend down to pet his cat. Horatio had always had very discerning taste in women, dismissing most of them without a second glance. Something about this woman obviously appealed to his cat.

Something about her appealed to Adam, too.

"Would you like a drink before we go?" he asked.

"No, thank you." She rose to her feet. "Where are we going?"

"They're having an anniversary party at the office. Nothing fancy. The first edition of *Adventurer* magazine hit the stands ten years ago today, so it's a great excuse to eat and drink on the company tab."

"How will you explain me?"

"Easy. You'll be there as my date."

She frowned. "Do I look like the type of woman you usually date?"

Far from it. He generally preferred redheads with IQs to match their bust size. Not cool blondes who made him think too much. Josephine Sinclair would stand out like a sore thumb at his office. Most of the staff were even younger than his advanced age of thirty, all twenty-somethings who liked to live on the edge.

"What kind of woman do you think I usually date?" he asked, evading her question with one of his own.

"Barbie doll-like women, but with bigger breasts," she ventured, coming closer to the truth than he wanted to admit.

He placed one hand over his heart. "I'm a man of taste. Refinement. I like all kinds of women, as long as they stimulate me intellectually."

Her eyes narrowed. "Really?"

"No, actually you got it right the first time. But it sounded good."

"Everything is a game with you, isn't it?" she said accusingly. "Even finding your so-called impostor. You're actually having fun."

"A life that isn't fun isn't worth living," he said, heading toward the door. He held it open for her. "Don't you agree?"

"Fun has its place." She stepped into the hallway. "I always schedule fun activities into my week."

"Schedule?" he said with a snort. They walked together toward the elevator. "Fun has to be spontaneous. Like when you climbed into my bed on Saturday night."

She stopped in front of the elevator. "I really wish you'd quit throwing that in my face."

He turned to look at her, inexplicably hurt by her

words. "I didn't say it to insult you. I really did have fun that night. And so did you."

The elevator doors slid open and she stepped inside. "I don't want to talk about it."

"I think we should talk about it," Adam said, joining her there. The doors slid closed and the elevator began its descent to the first floor. "Because that night seems to be a problem for you."

"A problem?" she echoed, her voice rising in the small elevator car. "How about a complete disaster?"

"I disagree."

"I don't remember asking for your opinion."

He pressed the Stop button on the elevator and it lurched to a halt. "Then I'll just have to prove it to you."

JOSIE STARED AT HIM for the space of three heartbeats. "What do you think you're doing?"

He took a step closer to her. "Are you afraid of me?"

"Of course not," she retorted, though her body prickled with awareness. The elevator was unbearably warm.

"Then you must be afraid of yourself."

"That's ridiculous!"

"Is it?" He reached out one hand and brushed his finger over her cheek. At her sharp intake of breath, he moved another step closer.

She didn't want to react this way, but every muscle in her body tensed as he lowered his head toward her mouth. Her back bumped against the wall of the elevator and a drop of perspiration trickled between her breasts.

But he didn't kiss her. He just stood there, his firm lips a hairsbreadth from her own. Their bodies didn't touch, but the air between them sizzled with heat lightning.

"You feel it, don't you, Josie?" he whispered, looking into her eyes.

She swallowed, wanting to deny it, but her body pulsed with molten desire as she remembered the last time he'd kissed her. The last time he'd touched her. Liquid warmth spread between her legs and, for a wild moment, she considered grabbing him by the collar and kissing him. Rubbing her body against him to ease the delicious pressure building inside of her.

Closing her eyes, she tried telling herself that he was just playing with her. That men like Adam used passion as a weapon—a weapon that could very well destroy her.

An alarm bell sounded, signaling that someone on another floor was waiting for the elevator. She opened her eyes at the noise and saw that he'd moved to a safer distance, acting as if the moment between them had never happened. She drew in a deep breath, then another, her mouth parched. Damn him for affecting her this way. She wasn't here for his amusement.

When Josie had calmed down enough to speak, she

met his gaze and said, "If you ever pull a stunt like that again, I won't help you."

She meant every word. Suddenly, exposure didn't seem like the worst possible consequence of her night with Adam. It would be mortifying, certainly, and something she wanted to avoid. But even worse than exposure would be losing her grip on her emotions. Letting a man like Adam run roughshod over her heart just for the fun of it.

He stared at her as if she was a puzzle he couldn't figure out. No doubt his other women enjoyed these kind of seductive games. Her stomach tightened when she thought of all the women who had probably shared his bed, then told herself she didn't care. How could she care when the man was practically a stranger to her?

Neither of them spoke again until they reached the penthouse office of *Adventurer* magazine. It was located in LoDo, the lower-downtown district of Denver that was known for having the trendiest restaurants, clubs and bars in the city.

The small reception area was filled with people and Adam lightly grasped her elbow as they stepped off the elevator. Her body tensed at his touch, but she could hardly pull away from him if she was masquerading as his date.

"Adam!" A buxom redhead barreled toward them, a tall, frosted glass in each hand. She looked barely legal and more than a little irritated that Adam hadn't arrived at the party alone.

"Hello, Shondra," he said.

Shondra held out a drink to him. "Welcome home. I made my great-grandmother's Irish iced tea just for the occasion."

"Thanks," he replied, taking it from her, then handing the glass to Josie. "This is my date, Josie Sinclair. Jo, this is Shondra O'Conner, the art director here at *Adventurer* magazine.

Josie smiled, gritting her teeth as Adam circled his arm around her waist. "Nice to meet you."

"Same here," Shondra said, staring openly at her. "So, when did you two start dating?"

Adam glanced at Josie. "Just after I got back from my trip."

"Tell me all about Rio," Shondra said, turning both her body and her attention toward him, effectively shutting Josie out of the conversation.

Josie took a sip of the iced tea in her hand, surprised at the strong kick of mint. She didn't much care for mint, but she was so thirsty it didn't matter. She took a second sip and let her gaze roam around the room.

Most of the people here looked younger than her twenty-seven years. More carefree, too. She supposed anyone who worked for *Adventurer* magazine wouldn't take life too seriously. Like Adam. At the moment, he was telling Shondra about parasailing in Brazil. The girl hung on his every word, gasping in horror when he mentioned almost crashing on top of a rocky cliff.

Josie wondered how much of his story was true and how much he'd made up to impress the girl. One thing was depressingly obvious. The man beside her really was Adam Delaney. Everyone in the room seemed to recognize him. Several people waved to him, a few raising their hands to give him a high five as they walked past.

Which meant her boyfriend, the man who had called himself Adam Delaney and who claimed he worked for *Adventurer* magazine, had been lying to her all along. Part of her had known the truth since the morning she'd awakened in Adam's bed. Another part of her still wanted to deny it. To prove that even if the deception was real, her boyfriend hadn't been using her. That if he'd deceived her, he'd done it for a good reason.

But she had to find him first.

She took another long sip of her minty iced tea, trying not to feel out of place. All the people here seemed to know each other and it just didn't seem possible that her boyfriend could be among them. Yet, Adam believed his impostor was someone he knew.

She slipped out of his grasp and began to wander around the reception area. Several people sent curious glances in her direction. No doubt they were puzzled by the woman Adam had brought with him to the party. Especially when a man like Adam could have any woman he wanted. That much was clear after the night she'd spent in his arms. He knew how to make a woman feel desirable and sexy. How to touch her with both longing and reverence. How to make a woman believe he wanted her and her alone.

But it had all been an illusion. He'd been making love to a stranger that night, not to Josie. Adam hadn't known her name or anything about her. Any woman would have satisfied him. Any woman at all.

She drained her glass, then crunched on an ice cube, pushing that night out of her mind. After skipping both lunch and dinner, she knew she should eat something, but the appetizers didn't look too appealing. She debated whether to try the sushi or the octopus salami, then decided to refill her glass with the mint tea instead.

Feeling a little more relaxed now, she took time to study her surroundings. Large photographic murals covered the walls. Scenes of jungles and mountains and deep gorges. Exotic places where Adam had probably traveled on his work assignments. Places that she'd only read about. As she circled the room, she heard snatches of conversations about skydiving and snorkeling. A harrowing encounter with a rampaging bull elephant in West Bengal.

She suppressed a shiver, then took another sip of her tea. These people seemed to thrive on danger, while she'd always done her best to avoid it. But listening to them made her wonder what she was missing. Her life seemed so narrow compared to the people around her.

Standing alone, Josie suddenly felt old and frumpy. She'd worn a dress suitable for a woman twice her age and had no exciting stories of her own to share with anyone. Unless you counted the time she almost got mugged one night outside the library. She'd been carrying a two-thousand page volume of A History of Human Civilization at the time and had smacked her unarmed attacker against the side of the head with it, dazing him enough to make her escape.

She could still remember the thrilling rush of adrenaline and the triumphant sense of exhilaration that had stayed with her for hours afterward. A feeling she hadn't experienced again—until Saturday night in Adam's bed.

Stop thinking about it, she admonished herself. Draining her glass, she filled it once again with the pitcher by the portable wet bar. She wasn't thirsty anymore, but felt more comfortable with something in her hands. Then she went in search of her date, bumping into a few people along the way, but none of them were Adam.

He wasn't where she'd left him by the elevator, either. Frowning to herself, Josie peered over the crowd of strangers, hoping he hadn't abandoned her here. Shondra seemed to have vanished as well. Maybe they'd left together.

"Greetings," said a voice behind her.

She turned to see a young man with a shock of orange hair spiked up all over his head. He wore black denim jeans and a neatly pressed black T-shirt with a skull and crossbones embroidered in orange thread on the pocket.

"Hello," she said, looking into his green eyes. They were nice eyes. Bright and friendly.

"I'm Paul Wodesky, but everybody calls me Woody."

"I'm Josie Sinclair," she replied, shaking his hand. "It's a pleasure to meet you."

"I was surprised to see you arrive with Adam. I thought he was coming solo tonight."

"Change of plans," she said, hedging, deciding not to elaborate.

Woody nodded. "So how did you and Delaney hook up?"

She sipped her iced tea, wondering how to answer that question. Telling him the truth was not an option. "We just sort of...bumped into each other."

"Cool," Woody replied, dimples popping up on both cheeks. "Delaney's a great guy. A little stiff sometimes, but hey, he did hit Highway 30 not too long ago. I'll be cruising there myself in a few years."

She blinked. Adam Delaney didn't strike her as stiff at all. Just the opposite. She opened her mouth to defend him, then closed it again. Why did she care?

"Nice threads," he said, looking down at her dress. "Very retro."

"Thank you." She took another sip of her tea, wondering if Adam had disappeared because he was embarrassed to be seen with her. She knew she probably stuck out like a thistle in a field of wildflowers. A tired thistle. She leaned against the wall. "So what do you do here, Woody?"

"I'm in research," he replied.

That sparked her interest. "Really? I do quite a bit of research in my own job. I'm a reference librarian at the Denver Public Library."

"No shit." He grinned. "Delaney and a librarian. Now that's what I call an intriguing combo."

She chose to ignore that. "What kind of research do you do?"

"Right now, I'm working on the history of hallucinogens in the aborigine culture. I find the subject fascinating, because hallucinogens are something of a hobby for me. Would you have anything at the library about it?"

"I'm sure I can thind something," she replied, her tongue stumbling over the words a bit. "I mean, *find* something."

"Cool," Woody exclaimed. "Maybe I'll stop by there sometime."

She nodded, then pushed herself off the wall. Her knees wobbled a bit and she took a moment to steady herself. Now Josie wished she had grabbed something for supper on her way over to Adam's apartment. She hadn't eaten much all day, her apprehension about this evening leaving her with little appetite. It was obviously catching up with her.

She politely excused herself from Woody, then walked over to the buffet table and helped herself to the safest offering—a handful of white cheddar crackers. She ate slowly, her tongue feeling oddly numb, then she washed the crackers down with her iced tea.

Still not feeling quite right, she went in search of the ladies' room, hoping to splash a little cool water onto her flushed face. Walking unsteadily down a long hallway, Josie realized she should have asked Woody for directions.

Her head began to spin as she opened door after door, finding empty offices instead of a bathroom. When she reached the last door, she leaned against it and closed her eyes, taking several deep breaths.

Maybe she was coming down with the flu. There had been a bug going around at work. Her stomach quaked, as if signaling it was about to reject the crackers she'd just eaten. She needed to find Adam and insist they leave.

Josie turned around and opened the door, disappointed to find yet another office. But this one had a small fountain in one corner. She walked over to it, one hand gliding along the wall to steady herself. Then she knelt down on the floor beside the fountain and splashed the tepid water onto her warm cheeks. It refreshed her a little. So did the breeze drifting in from the open doors of a balcony.

Rising slowly to her feet, she moved toward it, seeking some fresh air. She found a breathtaking view of the glittering Denver skyline. She also found Adam and Shondra.

The two of them stood with their backs to Josie, their heads bent close together and Adam's arm around Shondra's slender waist. The tender, intimate moment made her feel even more queasy.

"Excuse me," she blurted, whirling around too fast to keep her balance. She fell against the wall, then pushed herself upright again, determined to get as far away from them as possible.

"Josie," Adam called after her. "Wait."

She ignored him, racing blindly out of the office and down the hallway. Anger and disappointment pinched her throat and she couldn't figure out why. Adam Delaney meant nothing to her. So why was she reacting this way?

He caught her before she reached the elevator. "Where are you going?"

"Home," she said, aware of people staring at them. "I just want to go home. My Adam's not here."

"Okay," he said gently. "I'll take you home."

"No, I'll take a taxi," she replied, relieved when the elevator doors finally opened. "I don't need you."

"Yes, you do," he countered, bracing one broad arm around her waist to help her into the elevator. "You can hardly stand up."

She jerked away from him as the elevator doors closed. "I'm just tired."

A smile kicked up one corner of his mouth. "You're drunk."

"I haven't had a drink all night." She sagged against the wall. "Just tea."

He smiled. "Made with Irish whiskey and crème de menthe. That's one of Shondra's specialty drinks. She moonlights at the Alligator Bar just a few blocks from here and prides herself on using old family recipes."

Josie reached up and gingerly touched her cheeks and nose. "That explains why my face feels numb."

"A common side effect."

"Not for me." Her stomach roiled and apprehension skittered up her spine. She didn't like feeling this way, unable to control her own body. What if she got sick or passed out? Or worse, what if Adam tried to take advantage of the situation and seduce her?

Then again, why would he want her when he had a woman like Shondra waiting in the wings? He was probably eager to dump Josie so he could go back to her.

"I'll just take a cab home," she said, drawing back her shoulders and trying to regain her dignity. "You probably want to go back to the party."

"You have no idea what I want," he said huskily.

She met his gaze and felt dizzy again, but this time she couldn't blame the alcohol running through her veins. The temptation to reach up and feel the rough scrape of his whiskers against her palm proved too much to resist in her weakened state. Adam didn't move as her fingers trailed over his face, his body tensing at her touch.

What a gorgeous man.

"Gorgeous, am I?" he quipped, making her realize she'd said the words aloud.

Maybe she had more to worry about than getting sick or passing out. If she wasn't careful, she'd find herself climbing into his bed again. Backing away from him, she wondered if this elevator ride would ever end. Then she looked at the doors and realized they were standing open.

"When did we stop?" she asked, looking into the parking garage.

"A few minutes ago." He took her hand in his own and led her onto the pavement. "Can you walk?"

"Of course I can walk," she replied, belying her words a moment later by almost tripping over a small crack in the pavement.

Adam heaved a sigh of exasperation as he scooped her up in his arms. "You're something else, Jo."

"The name is Josie," she reminded him, feeling even more dizzy in his arms. "And I insist you put me down at once."

"It seems to me that you're in no condition to insist on anything."

They reached his car and he settled her into the passenger seat, then grabbed the seat belt and leaned across her body to buckle it.

She inhaled the spicy scent of his aftershave and felt the brush of his arm against her breasts. Her mind flashed back to their night together and the way he'd used his mouth on her breasts to drive her wild.

She leaned her head back against the seat and swallowed a moan.

"Are you all right?" Adam asked, concern knitting his dark brow as he pulled back to look at her.

"No," she replied, more to herself than to him. "I don't think I'll ever be all right again."

He smiled. "Shondra's Irish iced tea can have that effect on a person. Lucky for you, I know the secret cure."

"What's the cure?" she asked as he closed the passenger door then rounded the front of the Camaro and slid behind the steering wheel.

"You'll just have to trust me," Adam said, switching on the ignition. He wheeled out of the parking space, then headed toward the exit sign and down a long, narrow ramp at a speed that made her stomach reel.

How could she trust him when she wasn't even sure she could trust herself? She closed her eyes, telling herself the effects of the drinks would wear off soon.

If only she could say the same about the effect Adam had on her. He was worse than Shondra's iced tea, able to make her drunk with desire. She craved his touch, even knowing the addiction would only grow stronger if she gave in to it.

Which meant she had to find a cure for something else that ailed her—a bad case of lust. For Adam.

5

ADAM UNLOCKED THE DOOR to his apartment while Josie leaned heavily against the wall. "You should have let me carry you up here."

"I'm fine," she insisted, stumbling inside the apartment. She made it as far as the sofa, then collapsed onto the leather cushions.

He was surprised she was still conscious after ingesting three glasses of Shondra's potent Irish iced tea. Adam had learned the hard way not to indulge, especially when he was driving. Now he experienced a twinge of guilt for not warning Josie earlier.

She moaned softly, then looked up at him. "I still don't understand why you wouldn't just take me home. Or let me call a taxi."

Adam knelt down beside her, adjusting a chenille sofa pillow behind her head. Horatio lay on the back of the sofa, watching the two of them.

"Because you're in no condition to be on your own," Adam replied. "Besides, I told you I have the secret cure to prevent a hangover and all the ingredients are in my kitchen."

"Nothing with mint," she murmured, her eyes fluttering shut once more.

He smiled to himself as he rose to his feet. "Keep an eye on her for me, Horatio."

The cat blinked and Adam headed for the kitchen. He'd had the locks on the door changed this morning, but he still took the time to look for possible signs of an intruder.

At least he knew the impostor hadn't ripped him off—aside from swiping one old camera. Adam's private detective had let him know that this morning. Cole Rafferty's preliminary investigation showed that none of Adam's money had been touched and there were no other ominous signs that his impostor had set out to destroy him financially or ruin his career.

Even if he was harmless, the fact that Adam didn't know the man's identity frustrated him. At least now he could be assured that it wasn't one of his colleagues at *Adventurer* magazine. He'd been worried about that for a while, since it was obvious the impostor knew his work schedule. Otherwise, the guy wouldn't have cleared out of the apartment before Adam returned from his trip.

Yet, the impostor had left food behind in the cupboards, as well as those library books. Had he done it on purpose? Was this some kind of game to him?

More questions formed in his mind as he mixed the hangover remedy in a tall glass. Questions that would have no answers—until he found his impostor. There was a good chance Josie knew more than she was telling him. Now would be the perfect time to find out, since her defenses were wobbly.

He smiled to himself, remembering the way she'd caressed his jaw in the parking garage, along with her whispered confession that she found him gorgeous. Too bad she had to be drunk to admit it.

Adam carried the glass into the living room only to find Josie curled up asleep on the sofa. Her silky blond hair had come undone from the French braid and spilled over the sofa cushion. She lay with her hands folded under her cheek, her pink lips slightly parted. Unguarded and relaxed, she reminded him of a Botticelli angel.

He set the glass on the table, then grabbed his camera, overcome by the urge to photograph her like this. The steady click of the camera didn't wake her, letting Adam capture her from every angle.

Part of him didn't care if it did wake her. She'd be irritated, no doubt, but then he could photograph the emerald fire in her green eyes and the pretty pink blush that rose to her cheeks whenever he made her angry.

It had been too dark to see her the night he'd made love to her and now he wished that he'd turned on a light. Common sense told him that if he had, their night would have ended at that moment. Still, he craved to see her in the throes of sexual passion. To watch her expression as he touched her in just the right places and brought her to fulfillment.

When he ran out of film, Adam set down his camera. There were so many sides to Josie. So many images he wanted to capture so he could examine them at his leisure and figure her out once and for all.

Horatio jumped gracefully from the sofa to the coffee table, eager to sniff the contents of the glass that Adam had set there.

"Sorry, guy, that's not for you," he said, moving it out of the cat's reach.

Josie opened her lush green eyes at the sound of his voice, ending any impulse he might have about reloading the camera. She licked her dry lips before she spoke. "Where have you been?"

He sat down beside her on the sofa, then picked up the glass off the table. "All great inventions take time. Here, drink this."

She sat up, looking dubiously at the glass in his hand. "What's in it?"

He hesitated. "I think it's better if you don't know."

She took the glass from him, but still looked wary. "Something wildly exotic, I suppose. Like crocodile eggs or ostrich feathers."

Adam smiled. "Something like that."

"But no mint?"

"No mint," he promised. "No alcohol, either. And it's all natural."

"So is nightshade," she countered, sitting up on the sofa. "That doesn't mean it's safe."

"I left out the nightshade this time," Adam replied. "There's nothing poisonous in it at all. I promise. I also promise that if you drink this tonight, you'll feel much better in the morning."

She met his gaze, then released a sigh of resignation before raising the glass to her lips. Her nose wrinkled as she started to drink, but she didn't stop until she'd drained the glass.

Adam was impressed. Especially since the first time someone had brewed the concoction for him—made with tomato juice, an egg and a few other ingredients that added up to a vile combination—he'd spit out the first mouthful.

"That was awful." Josie shuddered, then handed him the glass. "Okay, I'm ready now."

"Ready?" he asked, arching an eyebrow.

"To go home."

He shook his head. "You're staying here tonight."

"That's not necessary," she replied, even as she sagged back against the pillow once more. "I'm perfectly capable of taking care of myself."

"Except that you can barely walk, much less drive. Besides, what if you have a bad reaction to the crocodile eggs?"

"The only bad reaction I'm going to have is a sore back if I sleep on this sofa all night."

"You're welcome to sleep in my bed."

Her eyes flashed. "Never again."

That sounded more like a challenge to Adam than a refusal. But no matter how much he was tempted, now was not the time to take her up on it. "You can sleep there alone. I'll take the sofa."

"No, I'll take the sofa," she said crankily, obviously willing to give up the battle to win the war. "I'll be fine here. You can go to bed now."

"All right," he said, pulling the cotton throw off the back of the sofa and settling it over her. "But before I do, I just want to tell you that you didn't interrupt anything on that balcony tonight. Shondra and I are just friends."

A blush washed up her neck. "Your relationship with Shondra is not my concern."

He slipped off her shoes, then tucked the blanket around her feet. "You seemed a little upset when you found us alone together."

She frowned. "Why would I be upset? I don't care who you seduce on a balcony."

"I was comforting a friend, not trying to seduce her. Shondra wanted someone to confide in about some problems she's having with her lover. Her *female* lover."

"So she went to an expert," Josie said dryly.

He bit back a smile. "Now you do sound jealous."

She met his gaze. "Let me make one thing clear. I have Adam—my Adam. I don't need or want any other man in my life. He's perfect for me in every way."

"Except he's not here," Adam retorted, irritated by the devotion he heard in her voice.

"If he *was* here, he wouldn't have let me get drunk. Or refused to take me home when I asked him. Or made me drink some vile concoction made with crocodile eggs or who knows what."

"If your lover boy was here," Adam interjected, his hands curling into fists, "I'd punch him in the nose."

"Now who sounds jealous?" she asked softly.

"The alcohol is making you delusional," he said gruffly. Then he leaned over her. "Good night, Jo."

She looked up at him, her green eyes wide. Adam heard a sharp intake of breath and knew she thought he was going to kiss her.

And she was right.

His gaze dropped to her mouth and he hungered to taste those lush pink lips again. But he steeled himself against the urge and placed a chaste kiss on her forehead instead.

"Sweet dreams," he whispered, before turning around and heading for his bedroom, certain he'd be having a few dreams of his own.

THE WATER TEMPTED HER almost as much as Adam. She hesitated on the sandy shore, tiny waves washing over her bare feet. Adam, his dark hair slick with water, stood in the *middle of the pond, holding his arms out to her. He was laughing and daring her to join him.*

Moonlight washed over her naked body and she stepped into the water, more to conceal herself from Adam than anything else. A delicious warmth surrounded her. She waded toward Adam, gradually heading into deeper water with each step. The water reached her hips then her shoulders.

She'd never been skinny-dipping in her life, but excitement tingled through her as she moved closer to him. The water was at her neck now. Adam hadn't moved, smiling confidently as he waited for her to come to him. But her feet began to drag, as if something was weighing them down.

Josie took another step, but there was nothing solid under her feet, just water. She went under, unable to move her legs enough to kick her way back up to the surface. Sinking down farther under the warm water, Josie wanted to yell for help, but she knew that was impossible.

She also knew Adam couldn't see her—that she had to save herself. But she couldn't seem to move her legs. She kept sinking, her arms waving wildly through the water.

Josie sat up with a gasp, her heart pounding in her chest. "A nightmare," she assured herself. "It was just a nightmare."

Yet, it had felt so real that terror still raced through her veins. Josie was an excellent swimmer, so why hadn't she been able to save herself in that dream? Then she looked down at her feet and saw Horatio sleeping on top of them. That accounted for the sensation of not being able to move her legs.

She dislodged the Siamese, prompting an irritated growl from him. Then she swung her legs to the floor and took a deep breath. Sunlight shone in through the window. She'd survived both the night and the nightmare.

"Good morning."

She glanced up to see Adam framed in the doorway of his bedroom. He wore flannel pajama pants and the same smile she'd seen in her dream. Daring. Inviting. Dangerous.

Josie rose to her feet. "What time is it?"

"Almost eight."

"Eight?" she echoed, not wanting to believe it. "It can't be eight. I'm always up every morning by seven."

"You had a late night last night," he explained, moving into the living room. "Along with three of Shondra's Irish iced teas. I'm surprised you woke up this early."

"I don't believe this," she said, running her fingers through her hair. "I have to be at the library by nine. And I still have to drive home to shower and change. I'll never make it in time."

"Can't you just call and let them know you'll be in a little late? Or better yet, take the day off. You probably still haven't completely recovered from last night."

"I feel fine," she retorted, then was surprised to find that it was true. No headache. No upset stomach. Though she did feel a little light-headed, that was probably due more to hunger than anything else. Adam's hangover cure had worked.

Everything else about him seemed to lead to disaster. Now he wanted her to walk in late to work or just skip it all together. As if the head librarian wasn't already suspicious that her personal life was interfering with her job.

"I take my work seriously, Adam. It's not a drop-in-when-I-feel-like-it kind of job."

"Then shower here," he suggested. "The library is only a few blocks away. That will give you plenty of time to get ready."

She hesitated, seriously tempted by his offer. Then she looked down at her wrinkled blue dress. "I can't wear this to work."

"I'll iron it for you," he offered. "Ironing is one of my many talents."

As much as Josie hated accepting his help, she hated the thought of arriving late for work even more. Besides, Adam had disrupted her life so much lately, he owed it to her. "I guess I don't have any choice."

"Is that a yes?"

"Yes."

He led her down the hallway to the bathroom. "There are clean towels in the linen closet, shampoo and soap on a shelf in the shower stall. Just give me a holler if you need anything else."

Josie stepped inside the bathroom and shut the door, locking it behind her. Then she began unfastening the row of buttons on the front of her dress, feeling a strange sense of déjà vu at stripping down to nothing in Adam's apartment.

A blush suffused her cheeks when she thought about the last time she'd taken off her clothes here. At least today wouldn't end in the same way.

She opened the door to the linen cupboard and saw a stack of neatly folded towels on one of the shelves. Her gaze drifted to the other shelves as she reached for a towel, noting the personal items he kept there. A bottle of expensive aftershave. A large tube of toothpaste. An economy-size box of condoms. She found herself wondering how long it would take him to use them all up.

It was a strangely intimate experience to glimpse what a man kept in his bathroom cupboard. A faint aroma of his aftershave lingered in the air and she took a deep breath, savoring the scent.

A knock on the door made her jump. Josie closed the cupboard door quickly, embarrassed to be caught snooping even if he wasn't aware of it. "Yes?"

"I need your dress."

She wrapped the towel tightly around her nude body, then cracked the door open a little to hand the dress over to him. "Here you go."

He took it from her as his gaze moved to the skimpy towel. "If you'd like some company in the shower, I'd be happy to wash your back."

She shut the door in his face and heard the sound of

his chuckle as she locked it once more. Adam seemed to thrive on making her uncomfortable. Well, two could play that game. She reached into the cupboard and grabbed his razor, feeling not the least bit guilty that she was going to use it to shave her legs.

Twenty minutes later, she stepped out of the shower feeling much better. Until she realized she didn't have anything to wear except her lace panties and bra. She rinsed her panties out in the sink, then dried them with his blow-dryer. Now, as she put them on, she wondered why she'd ever agreed to shower here in the first place. What if Adam refused to give her dress back? What if she had to parade around his apartment in her underwear to find it?

But when she cracked open the bathroom door, she was surprised to find her dress hanging on the door-knob. Swallowing a cry of relief, she grabbed it and closed the bathroom door once more. The dress was crisply pressed and even emitted a faint but pleasing aroma of lavender. The man was an enigma—mocking her with an offer to wash her back one minute, then carefully pressing her dress the next.

Josie didn't want an enigma in her life. She disliked mysteries or, more accurately, the uncertainties they presented. That was one reason she'd been drawn to her boyfriend. He'd seemed so...predictable. There had been a certain comfort in his predictability. Security. At least until she'd found out he'd been masquerading as another man.

Josie dressed quickly, applying makeup that she always carried with her in her purse, then sweeping her hair up into a loose chignon. Glancing critically at her reflection in the mirror, she wondered what Adam thought of her. She certainly wasn't as flashy as Shondra or as fashionable as most of the women she'd seen at the party.

"What do I care what he thinks?" she muttered to herself as she padded out of the bathroom and headed toward the living room. Though it was only eight-thirty, she was anxious to get away from Adam. All she had to do was grab her shoes and walk out the door.

Only her shoes weren't anywhere in sight. She knelt down to look under the sofa, but all she found there were a few dust bunnies. Kneeling on the living room carpet, she looked around the floor once more, wondering where they could be.

Adam appeared in the kitchen doorway, a dish towel slung over his shoulder. "Breakfast is ready."

"I'm not staying for breakfast," she informed him, rising to her feet. "But I can't seem to find my shoes."

"That's because I hid them."

She stared at him in disbelief. "You did what?"

His gaze slowly traversed her body all the way down to her bare feet. "You give me what I want, Josie, and I'll give you your shoes."

6

JOSIE COULDN'T BELIEVE her ears. He was blackmailing her—again. "I want my shoes, Adam, and I want them right now."

He didn't move. "I'll trade you one frittata for one pair of navy high heels."

She could see the amusement dancing in his brown eyes, but she didn't find it one bit funny. "You stole my shoes?"

"I needed them for leverage. You need to eat."

"I *need* to go to work."

He glanced at his watch. "You can leave here in twenty minutes and still arrive at the library in plenty of time for work."

"Not if I'm barefoot."

He smiled, then turned around and disappeared into the kitchen again.

She had no choice but to follow him there. "Did anyone ever tell you that you have serious control issues?"

"No one is perfect," he quipped, walking over to the stove and picking up a spatula off the counter.

"I mean it, Adam. First, you blackmail me into helping you find my boyfriend. Then you get me drunk, and then you steal my shoes. This is becoming a dangerous pattern."

"I didn't get you drunk," he countered, transferring a skillet from the stove to the table. He set it on a bronze trivet, loosening the thick frittata with the plastic spatula.

"You handed me that glass of Irish iced tea that Shondra gave you without bothering to mention that it contained more than tea!"

He nodded. "Okay, I'll concede that was a mistake. But I didn't do it to get you drunk. I thought it might help you relax a little. You seemed tense."

"I don't need to relax," she said between clenched teeth. "And that's a perfect example of what I'm talking about. You were trying to fix what you thought was wrong with me."

He met her gaze across the table. "I never said there was anything wrong with you."

"Please," she huffed, pulling out a chair and sitting down at the table. "I'm not exactly your type. So don't tell me there's not at least one or two things you'd like to change about me."

"You're right," he said, sliding a generous helping of the frittata onto her plate. "I'd like to see you smile more. And I'd love to hear you laugh. I don't think I ever have."

She picked up her fork. "Lately, there hasn't been

anything to smile or laugh about. Stealing my shoes *definitely* doesn't make me happy.''

Adam sat down across from her. ''I only did it because I knew you'd leave here without eating anything and you have to get something in your stomach. Like I said, I should have warned you about Shondra's Irish iced tea. I guess I feel responsible now.''

She arched an eyebrow. ''So you're fulfilling that responsibility by holding my shoes for ransom? Nice. Maybe for an encore, you can burn my house down. After all, the front steps are a little rickety. I might trip someday and sprain my ankle.''

He smiled. ''Always happy to be of service.''

She took a bite of the frittata, then almost moaned aloud at the delicious blend of eggs, cheese, vegetables and herbs. But she didn't want to give Adam the satisfaction of knowing how good it tasted. Or how ravenous she really was. Josie tried to slow down, but her omelet was half gone before Adam even took his first bite.

''Good?'' he asked, a knowing twinkle in his brown eyes.

''I just want my shoes,'' she hedged. ''You could put a pile of twigs on my plate and I'd eat them if it was the only way to get out of here.''

''I'm out of twigs,'' he teased. ''But I might have some bamboo shoots in the fridge if you have a craving for edible trees.''

Her mouth twitched and she reached for the glass of

orange juice in front of her. She wanted to maintain her righteous indignation, but it was difficult when he was doing such a good job of charming her out of her bad mood.

"Speaking of trees," he said, sprinkling some salt on his frittata, "have you ever been to The Pines Hotel out near Red Rocks Park?"

"No," she said warily. "Why?"

"Because there's an awards banquet there next Thursday night and I'd like you to come as my guest."

Josie stared at him. Was Adam Delaney asking her out on a date? Then common sense took over. "You think my boyfriend will be there?"

He nodded. "Everyone in the industry will be there. I think there's a good chance he could be among them. Especially since I think he did a lot of dabbling in my darkroom."

She turned her attention back to her frittata. "I'm sorry, I can't make it that night. I have other plans."

"Other plans?" Disappointment etched his brow. "Can't you change them? What could possibly be more important than finding my impostor?"

"I do have my own life, Adam." She finished the last of the frittata on her plate, then pushed it away. Pride prevented her from asking for seconds. "Thursday evening simply doesn't work for me."

"The banquet doesn't start until eight o'clock."

"My book club starts at seven and I'm sure it will run more than an hour."

"Book club? You're bailing out on me for a book club?"

"It's very important to me," she told him, a little wounded at his reaction. "It's a book club I initiated to study British authors and we meet every Thursday night after the library closes. We're discussing *Pride and Prejudice* by Jane Austen this Thursday, which happens to be one of my favorite books."

"I've never read it," he informed her. "But since it's been around for over a hundred years, couldn't you save the discussion for another meeting?"

"Absolutely not."

He set down his fork. "Are you sure there's not another reason you don't want to come to the banquet with me? Like maybe you don't really want to find your boyfriend?"

"That's crazy."

"Is it?" Adam leaned forward, as if he was onto something. "As long as my impostor remains invisible, you don't have to face the fact that the guy lied to you. Instead, you can just go on pretending that there's some reasonable explanation for his behavior."

"I want to find my boyfriend as much as you do," she replied. "No, even more than you do. I...care about him. A lot."

A muscle flickered in Adam's jaw. "I don't get it. He deceives you about everything, even his name, and you're still loyal to him."

"I just want to give him a chance to explain before I judge him." *A chance my father never got.*

He picked up his plate and moved to the sink. "It's almost nine. You'd better go."

She rose to her feet, a little surprised to find him giving in so easily. "I still need my shoes."

He opened the oven door, then reached inside and pulled out her shoes. "Here."

Shaking her head, she took them from him, slipped them onto her feet, then turned toward the living room. Horatio lay on the sofa, reminding her that she had something for him. She reached into her purse and pulled out the pink scarf the cat had snagged as she'd prepared to seduce her boyfriend. Adam had returned it to her, but Josie certainly didn't want any reminders of that night.

She tied it in a knot, then tossed it to the cat, who batted it in the air with one paw. Then she hesitated, wondering if she should tell Adam goodbye. He was still in the kitchen, the sound of water running in the sink.

Deciding it would be safer to leave without saying anything, she walked to the front door.

Adam's voice drifted out just before she stepped into the hallway. "I'll see you later, Jo."

It sounded more like a threat than a promise.

JOSIE ARRIVED AT HER LIBRARY desk at 8:59. She ignored the stares of her co-workers, who were used to finding her already working when they showed up. But she couldn't ignore Evelyn Myerson, who glanced at the wall clock then made a beeline for her desk.

"I have another phone message for you," the librarian said, adjusting her glasses.

Josie sat down at her desk, hoping it wasn't her mother again. "Oh?"

Evelyn handed her a note, then stood there while Josie scanned it. There was only one line.

Please don't give up on me.

Her heart lurched in her chest. Then she looked up at Evelyn. "That's it?"

The older woman nodded. "I asked the man if he wanted to leave a name or at the very least a telephone number where he could be reached, but he hung up before I could even finish the question."

It was from her boyfriend. It had to be. "What did he sound like?"

The director arched a thin eyebrow. "I'm not a voice expert. It was certainly no one I recognized."

"Yes, but did he ask for me by Josie or Josephine or Ms. Sinclair? Did he sound upset or afraid?" She was desperate for any details about him. Anything that might give her a hint regarding his whereabouts.

Evelyn crinkled her brow. "It was a very short phone call. Is there a problem, Josie?"

"No," she said hastily, aware that she'd probably revealed too much. "Not at all."

Evelyn nodded. "Good. Now if you'll excuse me, I'm sure we both have work to do."

But it was impossible for Josie to concentrate on anything but the note in front of her. Her boyfriend had finally made contact, though his message was both brief and puzzling.

Please don't give up on me.

She didn't want to give up on him, or believe he was as nefarious as Adam contended. Yes, he'd deceived her, but at least this was proof that he hadn't abandoned her as Adam had intimated earlier. If only her boyfriend had confided in her. If only he'd trusted her enough to tell the truth.

She cradled her forehead with her hands as a headache began to form behind her temples. Perhaps Adam's hangover cure was wearing off. Or the stress of the last few days was finally catching up with her. She'd tried so hard to maintain her normal life. To go on as if nothing had happened.

Please don't give up on me.

Why hadn't her boyfriend called her at home? She might have been able to talk to him. To at least discover his real name. Josie found she couldn't think of her boyfriend as Adam any longer. Not when the real Adam Delaney was so vivid in her mind. Every delectable inch of him.

She closed her eyes, remembering how he'd looked this morning with his hair tousled from sleep and dark whiskers thick on his jaw. He'd worn his pajama pants low on his hips, low enough for her to see the dark arrow of hair beneath his navel. It seemed impossible to believe she'd had her hands there—*and everywhere else.*

She sucked in a deep breath and opened her eyes. This wasn't getting her anywhere. Her boyfriend had finally made contact. That was a good sign. Now all she could do was wait until she heard from him again. If she was lucky, there was a message waiting for her on the answering machine at home. She'd check it during her lunch hour. Until then, she'd put her boyfriend, as well as Adam Delaney, out of her mind.

Before they both drove her crazy.

"YOU'RE IN BIG TROUBLE."

Those were the first words that greeted Adam when he walked into the front office of *Adventurer* magazine. Shondra was perched on the corner of the reception desk, eating a granola bar.

"Where's Lucinda?" he asked, referring to the office receptionist.

"Taking a late lunch," Shondra replied. "I'm covering for her."

"So why am I in trouble?"

"Don't ask me. Ask the big, bad boss. He left word he wants to see you the moment you set foot in this place."

"Maybe he wants to give me a raise. Or up my expense account."

"Keep dreaming." She popped the last bit of granola bar into her mouth, then licked her fingers. "Just a heads up—Ben is not in a good mood today. He didn't even laugh at my lawyer joke."

"That's because it's a lousy joke."

Shondra scowled at him. "You laughed."

"That's only because I'm a nice guy. But, as your friend, I'd advise you to stop telling jokes. You're really lousy at it."

She narrowed her eyes. "Well, since we're giving each other friendly advice, if I were you I'd watch out for that woman you brought to the party last night. She's trouble."

"Really?" he said, intrigued. "What makes you think so?"

"Call it woman's intuition." Shondra hopped off the desk. "I mean, let's face it, Adam, you've never had the best taste in women. How in the world did you ever hook up with someone like her?"

"It's a long story," he hedged. "And, for your information, I've got great taste in women."

She laughed. "Don't get me started critiquing your love life. Just take my advice and stick with dumb redheads. You'll be much happier."

He wanted to argue with her, but Ben Berger, the executive editor of *Adventurer* magazine, chose that moment to step out of his office.

"Lucinda, get that damn Delaney on the phone and..." He stopped when he realized the receptionist wasn't at her desk. Then he saw Adam and a look of palpable relief crossed his face. "Good, you're here. Can we talk, Adam?"

"Sure," he said uneasily. Ben wasn't into niceties. If he wanted to talk to somebody, he generally ordered them into his office. The uneasiness spread when Ben closed the office door behind them.

"What's the problem, Ben?"

"Please, have a seat."

Please? Now Adam knew he was in trouble. Ben never said please. The word simply wasn't in his vocabulary. Various possibilities for his boss's odd behavior flashed through Adam's mind. Was he about to get fired? Demoted? Assigned a photo shoot at the North Pole?

"Cigar?" Ben asked, holding out a box of his imported Cubans.

"No, thanks." Adam slumped back in his chair. He must have a fatal disease. Ben never shared his precious cigars with anybody, least of all his staff.

"I'm not sure quite where to start," Ben said, closing the cigar box and setting it on the corner of his desk. "I know you've always been honest with me, Adam, at least I hope you have. That's why the telephone call I received this morning disturbs me."

"Am I supposed to know what you're talking about?"

Ben met his gaze. "You better than anybody."

Maybe his boss had been dipping into Shondra's

Irish iced tea, because Ben wasn't making any sense. "Why don't you start from the beginning? Tell me about this telephone call you received."

"It was from Howard Walton at Empire Media. We're old friends, so he wanted to verify something he'd heard on the grapevine."

Ben paused, as if Adam was perfectly capable of filling in the rest. But he was still clueless.

"And?" Adam finally prodded.

"And he told me you're on the market." Ben leaned forward, resting his hairy forearms on his desk. "I wish you had discussed this with me before you started job hunting, Adam. If you're unhappy with your present salary or all of the traveling..."

"Wait a minute," Adam said, holding up both hands. "I'm not looking for another job. I'm happy at *Adventurer* magazine. Very happy. Although, I certainly won't argue if you want to give me a raise."

Ben scowled. "Then what's all this crap about you leaving for greener pastures?"

"I haven't the faintest..." The words died on his lips as the answer came to him. *The impostor.* He'd assumed the man had not interfered in his life in any meaningful way, but he'd been dead wrong. The guy was sending out his résumé!

"Hell," Adam muttered under his breath.

"You look like you need a drink," Ben observed, rising from his chair and heading toward the liquor cabinet.

"No, thanks." Adam needed to keep his head clear. He also needed to find his impostor before the guy did something to really screw up his life. "What I need is to find out how this rumor got started. Any clues?"

Ben shrugged. "Howard just told me your résumé has been making the rounds. He wanted to get in on the bidding."

That didn't sound too harmful, but how far had the impostor gone? Was he actually passing himself off to people as Adam Delaney?

"Tell me something, Ben," Adam said, watching his boss pour himself a double whiskey. "Anybody unusual around the office lately? Say, in the last three months?"

"You mean, other than Woody and the rest of the miscreants around this place?"

"Yeah. Like maybe somebody asking questions about me or my assignments."

The editor shook his head. "I can't think of anyone. Why?"

"Just wondering." He rose to his feet. "Look, I need to go."

"That's right," Ben said. "You've got to get ready for that photo shoot in New Zealand next week."

Damn. He'd forgotten to tell his boss that trip was off for a while. It was scheduled to last at least four weeks. Time he couldn't afford to take until he'd rendered his impostor harmless. "Look, I'm going to have to delay the New Zealand trip."

Ben frowned. "It's been on the calendar for months. We've got the photos scheduled for the September issue."

"I know. It can't be helped."

Suspicion once again flitted across his boss's face, but Adam didn't want to confide in him about the impostor. Until he knew the man's identity, he wanted to play this one close to his chest.

"How much time do you need?" Ben asked at last.

"I can't say for sure. One week, maybe two. Believe me, I'll be on the first airplane out of Denver as soon as possible."

Ben shook his head. "Damn it, Delaney, you'd better have a hell of a good reason for putting this trip off."

"I do," Adam replied, relieved to see the old, cantankerous Ben was back. "In fact, you could say my life depends on it."

Before Ben could ask him to elaborate, Adam was out the door and in search of some answers. He headed down the hallway and burst into Woody's office without knocking.

"Just in time," Woody said, nonplussed by his unexpected arrival. He handed over a digital camera. "I need you to take a picture of me."

"Now really isn't a good time," Adam said, then frowned down at the camera in his hand. "And this really isn't a good camera."

"I know, but this is an emergency."

"What kind of emergency?"

He grinned. "I just met this really cool girl on the Internet and she wants me to send her a picture. How do you like this pose?" He stood next to his computer, one hand resting on top of the monitor.

"The pose is fine, but the idea is crazy. What if she's one of those cyber-stalkers?"

"Hey, I believe in living dangerously. And so do you, judging by your date last night."

Woody was the second person who had referred to Josie as dangerous. "I see you've been talking to Shondra."

"Not just Shondra. Everybody around here is talking about that woman you brought to the party. I mean, she's not exactly your type."

"I don't have a type," he countered, growing a little irritated.

"So it's just a coincidence that your last four girlfriends have been intellectually challenged redheads?"

"I suppose your Internet girlfriend is a Rhodes scholar?"

Woody flashed a toothy smile. "She's not my girlfriend—yet. Now take the picture."

Adam sighed, then held the digital camera up to his eye. He adjusted the focus. "Say desperate."

"Horny," Woody said, his smile widening.

Adam snapped the picture, then handed him the camera. "Don't say I didn't warn you."

Woody sat back down at his computer. "I'm almost positive she's not a wacko. And despite Shondra's opinion, I don't think Josie is either. Man, she can really down those wicked Irish iced teas, though. Which makes her a lot braver than I am."

Adam had thought the same thing when she'd ingested the hangover cure in one big gulp. She didn't seem afraid of a challenge—just afraid of him.

Or maybe it wasn't fear, but something else. The same something that had made her refuse to accompany him to the awards banquet. That still bothered him, especially in light of the news that his impostor was making industry contacts using his name. Which brought him back to the original reason he'd barged into Woody's office.

"I need some information."

"Then I'm your man," Woody said, logging on to the computer. "What's the question?"

"This isn't about research," Adam replied. "I want to know if anyone unusual showed up here at the office while I was gone."

"Unusual is a relative term." Woody began to download his picture onto the computer. His digital image slowly appeared on the screen pixel by pixel. "Some people might even call me unusual. Can you be a little more specific?"

"How about a man asking questions about me? Or about my work?"

Woody thought for a moment, then shook his head.

"I can't think of anyone, other than that insurance guy."

"Insurance guy?"

"Yeah, he showed up right after you left for Brazil, trying to sell everyone on the staff a high-risk insurance policy. I told him you were the only one around here who would qualify as high risk, but that you wouldn't be back for at least three months."

Adam couldn't believe it. He finally had a lead. "What did he look like?"

Woody shrugged. "I don't know. Average, I guess."

"Come on, Wood, you've got to give me some details. Hair color. Eye color. Height. Weight. At least tell me if you've ever seen the guy before or since."

Woody leaned back in his chair, looking thoughtful. "To tell you the truth, Adam, he's not the kind of guy you notice much. Light hair, I guess. Maybe green eyes. Or gray. And like I said before, he's really just average. Not tall or short. Not skinny or fat. Average."

Adam swallowed a sigh of frustration. That narrowed it down to about a million people. But it was a start. And it reaffirmed the fact that his impostor probably wasn't anyone from *Adventurer* magazine, since this so-called insurance salesman had been a stranger to Woody.

"What's this all about, anyway?" Woody asked. "I've never seen anyone get so excited over insurance."

"It's a long story," Adam said, glancing at his

watch. "I need to run a few errands, so I'll have to fill you in later."

"And I'll fill you in on Miss Internet." Woody turned back to his computer, his image now on the screen in full color. He adjusted the color on his hair, toning down the orange. "Will I see Josie with you at The Pines on Thursday night?"

Josie had turned down his invitation to the banquet, but Adam was now more determined than ever to find his impostor, which meant he had to find a way to make her change her mind. "You can bet on it."

7

JOSIE COULDN'T PUT IT OFF any longer. The book club meeting had been scheduled to start fifteen minutes ago, but only half the chairs she'd set out in the private meeting room were filled. This was their third meeting and Josie was afraid it might be their last.

"*Pride and Prejudice* is thought by many scholars to be Jane Austen's finest work," Josie began, nervously clearing her throat.

For some reason she couldn't explain, the members of her book club just didn't seem to click. Maybe it was their eclectic backgrounds. The members included Helen, a retired math teacher, Ann, a legal secretary, a hairdresser named Tina, a female plumber's assistant who went by the name of Ronnie, a pregnant homemaker named Nancy and Giselle, who worked as a dental hygienist.

From all walks of life, these women shared a love of reading. But so far, their discussions had all been stiff and formal, not dissolving into the easy confidences that women with similar interests usually share.

They'd started out with twelve members and had dwindled down to six in just three short weeks. At this rate, her book club would fizzle out before it even really got started—something Josie couldn't let happen. This project was her baby, a chance to prove her skills at providing quality programs, and it had only gotten off the ground with her quiet persistence.

Evelyn had even hinted that if her book club proved successful, Josie could initiate more programs. She might even have a shot at filling the program director slot that was due to come open in six months. That meant a raise in salary and prestige.

But first, she needed to find some way to break the stiff formality that permeated the group. A common bond. Maybe they'd spent too much time analyzing the plots and characters and not enough time sharing how the stories had touched them.

"I have an idea," Josie announced. "Let's do something different tonight and kick off our discussion by going around the circle so each of us can share our favorite part of the book."

The group looked uneasily at each other, no one willing to start. Then the door to the meeting room opened and all heads turned in that direction. Josie stood up, more than ready to welcome another member to the group. But the moment she saw Adam's handsome face, the words of welcome froze on her lips.

"Hello," he said, flashing a smile as he walked toward the group. He was overdressed for the meeting, wearing a black suit and blue silk designer tie.

"What are you doing here?" Josie asked, shock making her blurt out the words before she could stop herself.

"Hoping to join in the discussion of *Pride and Prejudice*." He set down a shopping bag. "Have I missed anything?"

Giselle, the dental hygienist, patted the chair beside her. "We're just getting started. Please join us."

Adam took the seat next to her, smiling at the pregnant Nancy who sat on the other side of him. Nancy smiled back and quietly introduced herself. The rest of the group followed suit, talking more than they had at the last three meetings.

Josie stared at Adam, certain he was here to disrupt her meeting. He certainly didn't look like the literary type. More like a dark and dangerous hero in a gothic novel. No wonder the women in the group were practically swooning over him.

"This is Adam Delaney," she said stiffly, making his introduction to the rest of the group. "He's a photographer for *Adventurer* magazine."

"Isn't that exciting!" Tina exclaimed. "It's one of my favorite magazines."

Several other members murmured their agreement. Josie noticed that the young dental hygienist had scooted her chair a little closer to Adam's. She knew exactly why he'd shown up here tonight—to disrupt her meeting so she'd go with him to that awards banquet. Well, she wouldn't let him do it. Even if she had to embarrass him to stop him.

"Adam, we were just about to go around the circle and share our favorite part of *Pride and Prejudice.* Since you're new to the group, why don't we start with you?"

He hesitated. "I don't want to hog the spotlight at my first meeting. I'd rather just listen to what everyone else has to say."

"I'm sure we'd all like to hear your point of view," Josie persisted. "After all, you've traveled the world, photographing all kinds of people and places. You'll bring a unique perspective to our discussion."

Adam looked around the group. "Anyone else want to jump in here?"

The plumber's assistant cleared her throat. "Well, I enjoyed the parts with Mr. Collins. I can't believe Elizabeth's mother wanted her to marry that jerk."

"He was awful," agreed the math teacher.

"What do you think, Adam?" Josie asked, swinging the attention of the group back to him.

Adam nodded. "Mr. Collins was quite a character."

Josie tightened her jaw. He seemed perfectly at ease, despite her questions, and looked quite pleased at his attempt to throw her off balance. And he was doing a good job of it, too, judging by the way she was clenching the book on her lap.

She relaxed her hands, telling herself not to let him do this to her. She couldn't control Adam, only her reaction to him. Maybe if she simply ignored him instead of trying to put him on the spot, he'd get bored and go away.

"My favorite scene was when Elizabeth walked three miles in the mud to visit her sick sister at Mr. Bingley's house," Josie said. "I think that was a turning point for Darcy. He started to see her as someone to admire, even though Bingley's sisters strongly disapproved of her."

"It took Elizabeth longer to admire Darcy, though, didn't it?" Adam interjected.

She looked over at him, too surprised by his comment to respond. He'd obviously read the book or at least rented the movie.

"I mean, she was too enamored of Mr. Wickham to give Darcy a chance," Adam continued. "Wickham was an even bigger jerk than Mr. Collins, but she didn't want to see it."

"She had good reason to dislike Mr. Darcy at first," the pregnant homemaker said. "He snubbed her at the ball, saying she wasn't pretty enough for him."

"You can't always judge a person by first impressions," Adam said, his gaze still on Josie. "Elizabeth made that mistake with both Darcy and Wickham."

She cleared her throat, aware that he was talking about more than characters in a novel. "You make it sound as if Darcy was completely innocent in all of their encounters. Look how he proposed to her! He insulted her family and basically told her that he'd fallen in love with her against his will.''

''Right,'' Adam concurred, ''but one of the reasons she refused him was because she was still loyal to Wickham.'' He shook his head. ''I just don't get it. How could a woman as smart as her not see through his lies?''

Something told her they weren't talking about *Pride and Prejudice* anymore. But she was too caught up in the debate to stop now. ''Because she had no reason to distrust Wickham at that point in the story. When she did find out the truth about his background, then she looked at him differently. Do you think a woman should just give up on a man when she doesn't know the whole story?''

A muscle flexed in his jaw. ''I think some men aren't worth that kind of devotion. Wickham certainly wasn't. He deceived Elizabeth about who he really was from the start.''

''And she paid the price for it,'' Josie said softly. ''That mistake led to her sister running off with Wickham, which almost ruined their family.''

The legal secretary jumped in. ''Then Darcy came to the rescue.'' She sat back in her chair with a happy sigh. ''That's my favorite part of the book. When Darcy paid off Wickham to marry Lydia and saved the Bennet family from disgrace.''

''That was so romantic and a wonderful surprise,'' the math teacher said. ''Especially since Elizabeth thought Darcy was more disgusted with her family than ever."

Despite Adam's presence, Josie found herself enthralled with their discussion. Or maybe because it was happening at all. This was the most animated her book club had ever been.

"I think it was a surprise because Austen wrote the book from Elizabeth's point of view," Josie said. "We never really saw what Darcy was thinking. We could only judge him by his words and actions."

"And by Elizabeth's opinion of him," the math teacher said, "which changed drastically over time."

"Do you think that happens in real life?" Adam queried, still looking at Josie.

A blush warmed her cheeks. Did he really want her opinion of him to change? If so, he had a funny way of showing it. "Real life is seldom as neat and tidy as fiction."

"But messy can be fun," Adam countered. "Especially when you never know what's going to happen next." He rose to his feet. "In fact, I have a surprise of my own."

"Adam," she warned, sensing another disaster.

He ignored her, reaching into the bag next to his chair and pulling out a sleeveless black cocktail dress, beaded at the bodice and tastefully elegant in its simplicity.

"That's lovely," the retired math teacher breathed. "Just like something a movie star would wear."

"I'm hoping Josie will wear it to an awards banquet with me tonight. She's so dedicated to this book club that she didn't want to miss your meeting, but perhaps you won't mind if we cut out a little early."

"Of course not!" Nancy exclaimed before Josie could even open her mouth. All the other members of the group joined in a chorus urging Josie to leave with Adam.

He'd put her in an impossible position and he knew it. Adam had charmed the group within the first five minutes of his arrival. He'd brought new life to their book club, transforming it with a lively, open discussion. If she turned him down, she'd look rude and petty. Worse, it might be the deathblow to the project she so desperately wanted to succeed.

But at least she could make him pay for it. "I'll go if Adam promises to attend our book club meeting every week from now on."

He flinched a little, but recovered nicely. "I can't think of anything else I'd rather do."

"Good," she said, smiling sweetly on the outside, but raging on the inside. "Next week, we're discussing *Wuthering Heights* by Emily Brontë. I can't wait to hear your thoughts."

"And I can't wait to hear yours," he replied, handing her the dress.

"Oh, you will," she promised. "You will."

"OF ALL THE DIRTY, underhanded tactics," Josie huffed as she emerged from the staff lounge of the library.

She'd gone there to change while the rest of the book-club members had slowly dispersed. The library closed at five-thirty on Thursdays and Fridays, so Adam and Josie were the only two people in the building.

Adam opened his mouth to respond, but the words died on his lips. She looked incredible. The dress hugged her figure, revealing generous curves that she tried so hard to conceal beneath those shapeless suits she wore.

"Wow," he breathed. It was all he managed to get out.

She stopped in her tracks, then looked down at the dress. "It's too snug."

"It's perfect," he replied, his gaze falling to her generous cleavage.

"How did you know my size?"

Blood slowly flowed back up to his brain. "When I ironed your dress the other day, I happened to notice the size on the tag."

"So ironing my dress wasn't just an act of kindness," she said with a frown. "You had ulterior motives."

"Not at the time," he replied honestly. Adam couldn't seem to stop staring at her. He even found himself now admiring the way she wore her hair up, noting the lean, graceful column of her neck.

"Well, you certainly had ulterior motives tonight."

She marched toward the front entrance. "I can't believe you ambushed me like that. You knew I couldn't refuse you in front of my group."

"I was just hoping to change your mind," he countered, following her out the door. His gaze fell to the sway of her round hips and for a brief, lust-filled moment he forgot where they were going.

"As if I had a choice!" She waited impatiently for him to walk through the door, then reached her hand inside to flip off the last bank of lights. Darkness blanketed the interior of the library as she closed the door, then twisted a key in a heavy dead bolt lock.

He found himself enjoying her heated tirade almost as much as he enjoyed the sight of her in that dress. Her chest heaved with each word, pressing her breasts against the low-cut bodice. He definitely approved of the dress he'd chosen.

Just as he approved of his new taste in women.

"Are you even listening to me?" she challenged, planting her hands on her hips. A car alarm blared down the street, but she either didn't notice or didn't care.

"Every word," Adam vowed. "Josie, I know you're upset. But I have every right to be upset, too—since your boyfriend seems intent on destroying my life."

His words seemed to diffuse some of her rage. "What do you mean?"

"My boss called me into his office yesterday and

told me someone is applying for jobs under my name. I'll give you three guesses on who that someone must be."

She licked her lips, obviously trying to come up with a credible excuse. Her automatic response to defend her missing boyfriend made him want to find a way to drive the man out of her mind.

"That hardly sounds like ruining your life," she said at last. "Maybe it's just a...misunderstanding."

"You're too smart to play dumb," Adam retorted. "Obviously, your boyfriend's masquerade was more than a lark. He's still passing himself off as me. I want to know why and I want to stop him before he does some real damage."

"No matter what the cost?"

They still stood on the front step of the library, the warm evening breeze loosening Josie's chignon so that curling wisps of blond hair now framed her face.

Damn, he wanted to kiss her.

Adam had been able to resist temptation when she played cool and aloof, but she was anything but cool now. Emerald fire lit her beautiful green eyes. She had no clue how much he desired her—and how much he wanted her to see the truth about her so-called boyfriend.

"No matter what the cost," he said. Then Adam turned around and headed for his Camaro, wishing like hell he'd never met her. Ever since the night she'd climbed into his bed, his life hadn't been the same.

Maybe it never would be again.

"This is it, Adam," she said, following him to the curb. "This is the last time I let you drag me somewhere I don't want to go."

"Why?" he challenged, opening the passenger door of his car for her. "Afraid?"

"Of course not!"

"Are you sure? Maybe you're afraid to find out the truth about your boyfriend." His grip tightened on the door handle. "Or maybe you're afraid of me."

She stood inside the car door, one hand braced on the window frame. Her mouth was so close, he could lean in and kiss her before she could even react. But Adam wasn't into sneak attacks—although his arrival at her book club meeting tonight might qualify as one.

"I'm not afraid of you," she breathed, though her eyes told a different story. He saw a hint of panic there. And excitement. Maybe she wasn't as angry at him as she sounded. Or was that just wishful thinking?

"Good," he replied, surprised to discover how much he wanted it to be true. How much he wanted *her.* "Because I'm not going to force you into anything. You can walk away now, Josie. I'll find your impostor boyfriend on my own."

She hesitated, and for a brief moment he feared she would take him up on his offer. At last, she shook her head. "I've already come this far, I may as well see it through to the end. I want to find my boyfriend as much as you do."

That was the last thing he wanted to hear. When she seated herself in the car, he pushed the door shut, all sorts of unsettling thoughts running through his head. What if finding his impostor meant losing Josie? What if she actually went back to that lying jerk?

Just the thought of her in another man's arms made his gut clench. The reaction surprised him. He'd never been the jealous type. Especially when the woman didn't even *like* him.

Maybe it was time he did something about that. Just like Darcy had won over Elizabeth. It would certainly make their search for his impostor more enjoyable. And he wouldn't have to worry about her running back into that jerk's arms—not if Adam kept her happy in his bed.

But first he had to come up with the perfect plan.

THE PINES HOTEL sat nestled in the foothills of the Rocky Mountains near Red Rocks Park, fifteen miles outside of Denver. The Red Rocks, natural red sandstone monoliths, rose to dramatic peaks around the hotel. An open-air amphitheater with perfect acoustics made Red Rocks a frequent site of outdoor concerts, so The Pines regularly hosted musicians and artists from all over the globe.

Josie felt as if she were stepping into another world when she walked into the grand ballroom on Adam's arm. She wished now she'd taken more time with her hair and makeup while changing into her dress.

"This is it," Adam said, as they mingled among the crowd. "The biggest bash of the year for the outdoor magazine industry."

She noted a few famous faces among the crowd, as well as more than one envious glance cast her way. But Adam seemed oblivious to the glamorous women surrounding them, focusing all his attention on her.

He bent his head toward her. "Have I told you how great you look in that dress?"

"Only two or three times."

He smiled. "Believe me, it's worth repeating."

Josie wished she could stay angry at him—she'd been so annoyed with him earlier, she hadn't even bothered to tell him about the phone message she'd received at the library. But now she was beginning to enjoy the evening in spite of herself. They found the table reserved for the staff of *Adventurer* magazine, though none of the others had arrived yet.

"Shall I get us something to drink?" Adam stood with her at the table, the pressure of his palm warming the back of her waist.

"That sounds good," she replied, fully recovered from the last party. "Anything but Irish iced tea."

He chuckled. "How about a glass of wine?"

"Perfect."

"What kind?" he asked. "Merlot? Maybe a nice chardonnay?"

"Surprise me."

He lifted his eyebrows. "I thought you didn't like surprises."

She met his gaze and an unexpected thrill of anticipation shot through her. "They're starting to grow on me."

He looked around the empty table. "I don't want to leave you here alone. Woody should be around here someplace."

"Don't worry about me," she assured him. "I'm going to do a little exploring. I've never been to The Pines before."

He nodded. "Then shall we meet back here in a few minutes?"

"All right," she agreed, then watched him walk toward the bar. He didn't even make it halfway before he was intercepted by a group of young men. Everyone here seemed to know him, which meant it would take him a while to work his way to the bar.

That would give her the time she needed.

Josie headed out of the ballroom and made a beeline for the hotel gift shop. After paying outrageous prices for a miniature bottle of styling gel, she found a ladies' room and applied eyeliner, blush, mascara and lipstick. Then she loosened her hair from its neat chignon and ran a comb through it. Squirting styling gel into her palm, she rubbed her hands together, then flipped her head upside down and ran her fingers through her hair.

She straightened once again and looked in the mirror, seeing that her natural blond curls had come to life. The expensive gel gave her hair a sexy, tousled look that was perfect for the occasion.

Now she was ready to join the party.

Stepping out of the ladies' room, she took a moment to get her bearings, then headed back to the ballroom. She stood at the top step of the entrance, searching for Adam. He wasn't at the table yet, though she saw Shondra sitting there with another woman.

Josie's gaze slowly scanned the ballroom, stopping when she saw the back of a man in a tuxedo. He didn't seem as broad at the shoulders as Adam or as tall, yet something about him nagged at her. Then he turned around and she realized why he looked familiar.

She'd found her boyfriend.

8

ADAM COULDN'T FIND his date anywhere.

He threaded his way through the crowded ballroom, absently waving to friends and acquaintances. He'd waited at the table for her, but with the ceremony due to start at any moment, he'd abandoned it to search for her.

Maybe she'd gone home. It would probably serve him right after tricking her into coming with him this evening. Yet, what choice did he have? He had to identify his impostor and put a stop to all the chaos. Three editors from magazines around the country had left messages on his answering machine in the last two days, expressing interest in hiring him.

Adam had turned them down, but feared it wouldn't end there. The jerk had already screwed up his travel schedule. After all, Adam couldn't take the chance of leaving the country for New Zealand and allowing the man to take over his life once more.

"Hey, Delaney," barked a voice behind him. He turned to see Lou Bailey, the owner of the biggest photography store in Denver. Bailey had sponsored several exhibits that Adam had participated in and they'd been friends for almost five years.

"Good to see you again," Adam said, holding out his hand.

Lou didn't take it. "I wish I could say the same. But I'm still waiting for you to pay for that two-thousand dollar camera you charged to my store, along with all that other equipment."

"I didn't buy...." His voice faltered. The impostor had struck again.

"Look," Bailey continued, trying to sound reasonable despite the undercurrent of anger in his tone, "I only offered you store credit because I thought you were a man of your word. But I'm not a damn bank. I have my own bills to pay."

"Didn't you know it wasn't me?" Adam asked, wondering if the impostor was a master of disguise. Josie had claimed the two of them looked nothing alike.

"Wasn't you?" Bailey said, scowling. "You came into the shop with one of my credit vouchers made out in your name. I wasn't there, but I'm sure my employee will verify its authenticity."

The impostor had infiltrated his files after all. And used the credit voucher Bailey had given him to go on a wild spending spree.

"Don't worry, Lou, I'll pay any and all outstanding bills," Adam vowed. "I apologize for the mix-up. It won't happen again."

"I hope not." Bailey looked more disappointed than angry now. "You've got a good reputation in this town, Delaney. Across the country, for that matter. I'd hate to see you do anything to ruin it."

Bailey disappeared into the crowd before Adam could respond. He looked around the ballroom, wondering how many other people he owed money. This problem was becoming bigger every day. If he didn't find his impostor, he'd have to spend the rest of his career doing damage control.

If he still had a career.

The lights in the ballroom dimmed and the activity on the stage signaled that the ceremony was about to begin. He still didn't have a clue where his date had gone. Though tempted to continue his search for her, Adam headed back toward the table, more frustrated than ever.

He couldn't find his impostor and now he couldn't even find his date. Yet his gut instinct told him she'd show up eventually. Just like it told him he could trust her.

He hoped he wasn't being a fool.

JOSIE WALKED UP to the man she hadn't seen in several days, still too shocked to speak. He carried a tray on his left arm, oblivious to her as he picked up empty glasses off a table.

Then he turned and saw her standing in front of him.

The tray tilted to one side, the glasses sliding precariously toward the rimmed edge. He balanced the tray just in time to avoid a disaster.

Then he blinked at her, his Adam's apple bobbing in his throat. "Josie?"

"Where have you been?" she asked, finding her voice at last.

"Wow." He looked her up and down. "You look fantastic."

"You haven't answered my question." Josie wanted to reach out and shake him by the lapels of his waiter uniform. Instead, she sucked in a deep breath and waited for him to stop gaping at her.

He slowly shook his head. "This is quite a shock."

"For both of us."

He moved in closer, lowering his voice to a husky whisper. "I've missed you so much."

"Then why didn't you call? Or write?" Her voice was rising with each word. "Or even send me an e-mail? All you did was leave that cryptic message at the library."

He hesitated, then gently grasped her by the elbow. "Come with me. I can explain everything."

She let him lead her across the ballroom and into the bustling kitchen. Her heart pounded in her chest, knowing this was the moment she'd been waiting for since waking up in Adam's bed almost a week ago. The moment she'd finally understand why the man

she'd seriously considered marrying had masquer-
aded as Adam Delaney for the last few months.

Chefs and waiters stared as he led her into a large
pantry, then shut the door behind them. It was dim
and cool inside, the bare lightbulb casting shadows all
around them.

He set down his tray on an empty shelf, then he
pulled her into his arms. "I'm so happy to see you
again, Josie. You look incredible."

She let him hold her, loosely circling her arms
around his narrow shoulders. The difference in size
between her boyfriend and Adam made her wonder
once again how she could have ever mistaken the two
of them, even in the dark. But now wasn't the time to
dwell on that mistake. She wanted answers.

When his embrace grew more intimate, Josie pulled
away from him. "What's going on?"

He sighed deeply, shaking his head. "There's so
much to tell you. I'm not even sure where to begin."

At least he was willing to talk to her. She'd half expected him to bolt the moment he saw her. "Let's start
with your real name."

"It's Lance," he said sheepishly, taking her hands in
his own. "Lance Golka."

"Why did you lie to me, Lance?"

He closed his eyes, gently squeezing her hands.
"Oh, Josie, I've made so many mistakes! The worst
was not telling you the truth from the beginning."

She knew she should feel relieved by his apparent

remorse. Since he'd gone missing, she'd worried that her boyfriend had simply been playing her for a fool. That he didn't care about her at all. The thought that she could misjudge him so badly had unsettled her. But he seemed much like the man she had known before. Only now she found herself wondering what she'd ever seen in him.

"Then please tell me what's going on," she implored, knowing they didn't have much time. "I want to know everything."

"Adam and I go back a long time," Lance began. "We were college roommates at the University of Colorado. Both photographers for the college newspaper. He was majoring in pre-law and I was an English major."

Josie still couldn't see Adam as a stodgy lawyer, though he seemed capable of charming his way out of any situation. Lance lacked the same charm, but he at least he seemed sincere.

The pantry door swung open and the head waiter frowned at Lance. "It's not break time yet, Golka."

"Yes, sir, I'll be out in a minute."

The head waiter glanced at Josie, then straightened his bow tie before disappearing into the kitchen once more.

"Anyway," Lance said, turning back to her, "during our senior year, I started wondering if I was making the right choices. I loved photography, but I didn't think I could actually make a living at it. Of course, no one bothered to tell me that an English major doesn't have employers lining up to hire him, either."

"What does this have to do with Adam?" she asked, not sure where he was going with this story.

"Adam was all set to go to law school," Lance replied. "He'd even been accepted to Yale. Then I told him about a photography contest I was going to enter. Top prize was a thousand dollars and a chance to interview for a job with some of the top magazines in the country."

"So Adam entered the contest himself and won the prize you thought you deserved," Josie guessed.

"Yes and no," Lance replied. "You see, I never entered the contest. I figured I couldn't win anyway, so why bother?" His face darkened. "But I never thought Adam would enter. He had his life all mapped out."

"I don't understand," Josie said, even more confused by his story. "That all happened years ago. What does it have to do with you taking over Adam's life?"

"Because Adam has the life I should have had if I'd just had the guts to go for it!" Anguish shone in Lance's blue eyes. "I got laid off six months ago, Josie. From a used-car dealership. Can you believe I couldn't even make it as a used-car salesman?" He shook his head in disgust. "That's when I started thinking about Adam. About how his life had turned out so perfect because of that contest. The guy is living *my* dream."

"Oh, Lance," Josie said, the name unfamiliar on her lips. He was like a stranger to her. She felt only pity and disappointment, not longing or even attraction to the man she'd been ready to give her heart.

"You probably think it's crazy," Lance said, dropping her hands, "but I've been following every step of Adam Delaney's career since college. I know everything about him. So I just wanted to see what it was like to be him. To live his life for just a little while. No harm done."

"I wish that was true," she whispered, thinking about the night she'd spent with Adam. Lance had no idea of the consequences of his actions.

He sighed. "You're right. I hurt you." He took a step closer to her. "I'm so sorry, Josie. That was never my intention. I was trying to work up the nerve to tell you everything when you took off for Tempe. Then Adam came back to Denver sooner than I expected and everything just fell apart. I barely made it out of his apartment in time."

"You should have found some way to warn me that you weren't there," she said, knowing it wouldn't have done any good. She'd gone straight to Adam's apartment from the airport.

"Please say you'll forgive me, Josie," Lance implored, moving even closer. "That you'll give me another chance. I might have lied about my name and my identity, but I never lied about my feelings for you. You are the only good thing to come out of this mess."

"Lance, I..."

The head waiter stuck his head through the door. "Time's up, Golka."

"Okay, I'll be right there." He turned back to Josie. "Well?"

She didn't know what to tell him, so she changed the subject. "Adam is looking for his impostor and I'm the only one he knows who can identify him. He brought me here tonight for just that reason."

Lance blanched. "You mean Adam knows that I'm here?"

"No," she replied. "He doesn't even know *you're* the impostor. But he believes it might be someone he knows in the industry. That's why he thought there was a good chance his impostor would be here tonight. But among the guests, not the waiters."

"He was right," Lance said grimly. "Because after tasting Adam's life for three short months, I know that's what I want now. That's the reason why I hired on here tonight. I was hoping to make some contacts."

"Maybe Adam could help you," she suggested, though she doubted he'd be that generous.

"Or throw me in jail," Lance said wryly. "Look, I need to find a chance to explain everything to him in my own time and my own way. A chance to make amends. But there's no way I can do that unless..."

"Unless what?" Josie asked warily.

"Unless you keep my secret."

ADAM BREATHED A SILENT sigh of relief when Josie finally appeared at their table. She hadn't abandoned him after all. He stood up to pull out her chair, still bothered by his conversation with Bailey. The more he thought about his impostor, the more frustrated he became.

He leaned down near her ear, barely aware of the speaker on the stage announcing the nominations for best editor. "Where have you been?"

She glanced up at him. "I...lost track of time."

"I thought you might have gotten lost or..."

"Left?" she ventured.

He sat down beside her. "I'll admit the thought crossed my mind. But I knew better."

"Good." She reached for her wineglass. "I'm sorry I took so long. I decided to touch up my makeup and do something a little different with my hair."

"You look lovely," he told her.

Her tousled curls reminded him of how she'd looked the morning after he'd made love to her. All rumpled and sexy and gorgeous. Now he was more determined than ever to romance her back into his bed. Unfortunately, now wasn't the time or the place.

"Any sign of my impostor?" he asked.

She choked on her wine, grabbing the linen napkin in front of her and raising it to her mouth. All the occupants at the table turned to look at her.

"Don't get all choked up on my account," Ben Berger told her. "I always get nominated and never win. I'm the Susan Lucci of the magazine world."

The fifty-five-year-old editor had brought a twenty-one-year-old intern as his date and was trying his best to look young in a black leather jacket. Only his ill-fitting toupee ruined the effect.

"Oh, I love Susan Lucci," Ben's date gushed. "I hope I can look as good when I'm her age."

"Yeah, she's getting up there." Shondra said and grinned at Ben. "How old is she now? Around fifty?"

Ben ignored her, turning to Adam. "Aren't you going to introduce me to your lovely date?"

Adam made the introductions around the table, though he knew Josie had already met some of them at the office party. Most of them had brought dates along, though Woody was flying solo tonight, still enamored with his long-distance love on the Internet.

As the nominations for best graphic artist were announced, Adam leaned over to whisper in her ear. "I hope this isn't too boring for you."

"Not at all," she replied, her warm breath caressing his cheek. "I've never been to anything like this before."

He sighed. "I just wish I could enjoy it."

Her brow furrowed. "Is something wrong?"

"I guess this whole impostor nightmare is finally getting to me. When I find out who he is, I'm going to wring his scrawny neck."

She flinched, then turned her attention back to the

stage. Adam wanted to kick himself. Telling her he wanted to inflict bodily harm on her boyfriend probably wasn't too bright, especially since she was still devoted to the guy. Maybe he'd better just shut up and enjoy the view.

He watched her settle back in the velvet padded chair, admiring once again how damn good she looked in that dress. But it was more than her looks that appealed to him. He'd taken out scores of beautiful women, so many he couldn't even remember all their names. But Josie had something more.

She possessed a keen intelligence that both challenged and amused him. She didn't seem impressed by his credentials, either, which was a refreshing change from the women he usually dated. Too many were aspiring models who cared more about making the right business connections than discovering the real Adam Delaney.

Now he realized he was interested in finding out more about the real Jo. Her interests and hobbies. Her friends and family. He already knew one of her favorite books. What else did she like?

Josie turned to him, unaware of his scrutiny, her finger pointing to an item on the program. "You didn't tell me you were up for an award."

He shrugged, not able to take his eyes off her face. "I guess I forgot about it."

She arched a blond eyebrow. "What exactly is the Insanity Award?"

Woody laughed at her question. "*Adventurer* magazine has a lock on that particular award every year, thanks to Adam."

"So what is it?" she asked again.

Shondra answered before Adam had a chance. "It's an award for the photographer or reporter who takes the biggest risks to get a picture or story."

"What kind of risks?" Josie asked.

"Well, let's see now," Woody mused, rubbing his chin. "There was the time Adam went scuba diving in alligator-infested waters for an underwater shot."

"Or how about the time he went skydiving over the Sahara desert at sunset," Shondra added. "Now that was a cool picture."

"My favorite was the shot from the top of Mount Everest," Ben remarked. "Did you know that twenty percent of the people that attempt a climb to the summit of Everest never make it back down?"

"Any professional would do the same," Adam said, a little embarrassed to have his career exploits paraded in front of Josie. It almost sounded like he'd put them up to it just to impress her.

Shondra rolled her eyes. "Right—and any other professional would likely get killed in the process. That's why you're the best."

"So which of those pictures got you nominated for the Insanity Award?" Josie asked him.

"Oh, those were all previous years' winners,"

Woody explained, his mouth curling up in a grin. "Tell her about this year's picture, Adam."

"It's just a shot off a bridge," he replied.

"And?" Shondra coaxed.

He frowned at her. "And I needed to get a decent angle, so I used a suspension rope."

"What he isn't telling you," Ben said, casually draping his arm around the back of the intern's chair, "is that Adam was hanging from the suspension rope at the time. Over a hundred and fifty feet below the bridge. A bridge that spans a gorge over a mile deep."

Josie paled. "That's insane."

"Thus, the name of the award," Woody quipped. "And why Adam's a perennial favorite to win."

She turned to look at him. "No job is worth those kinds of risks."

"Hey," Ben interjected gruffly, "let's not have that kind of talk."

"I'm not doing it for the job," Adam told her, wanting her understand. "I'm looking for the perfect shot. The one picture that captures the...magnificence of life. I still haven't found it. Maybe I never will."

"Or you'll die trying," she said softly.

Adam was touched by the concern etched on her face. Did she actually care about him? "I don't have a death wish," he assured her. "In every one of those shots, I utilized all kinds of safety precautions."

She leaned closer, curiosity lighting her eyes. "So what did it feel like hanging over that gorge?"

"Indescribable," he replied. "That's why I can't imagine doing anything else with my life. Photography is my passion. Seeking the perfect shot is what makes me want to get up in the morning and it's what I dream about at night. Every day is a new adventure."

"So you've never had any regrets about your life?"

"Regrets?" he echoed, confused by the question. "No. Not once. Why should I?"

Her shoulders moved in a slight shrug. "Some people don't follow their dreams. They take the safe route instead, then always wonder what might have been."

"Do you have regrets?" he asked, truly curious. What were Josie Sinclair's secret desires? What motivated her to get up in the morning? What filled her dreams at night? Adam found himself wanting to fulfill every one.

"Sometimes," she replied, "I love my work at the library, but I'd like to see the world someday. But, actually, I was thinking of...someone else." Her voice trailed off as she looked up at an approaching waiter.

Adam glanced at the man, then did a double take. "Lance? Lance Golka?"

His old college roommate grinned. "At your service."

9

JOSIE STARED UP at Lance, amazed by his audacity. She'd half expected him to flee the building after she'd told him Adam was here. Then again, Lance must have known Adam would be at this awards ceremony before he'd even taken the job. Had he planned it this way all along?

"Hey, what are you doing here?" Adam asked, rising to his feet and pumping Lance's hand.

"Making a few extra bucks," Lance replied. His gaze moved to Josie, then back to Adam again. "I see you're still working for *Adventurer* magazine."

"They haven't fired me yet," Adam said with a grin. "How about you, Lance? I haven't seen you for years. Not since we graduated college."

"Oh, I dabble in a little bit of everything," Lance replied. "I'm working on a novel."

"The same one you started in school?" Adam asked.

Lance nodded. "That's right—my magnum opus. It's slow going, but the great ones always are."

Adam turned to Josie. "This is Lance Golka, my roommate from Colorado U. Lance, this is my date, Josie Sinclair."

Josie rose to her feet, her knees shaking. Now was the time to come clean. To tell Adam that his impostor stood right in front of him. But she made the mistake of looking into Lance's eyes. They were filled with apprehension, silently pleading with her to keep his secret.

"Nice to meet you," Lance said, reaching out his hand.

She shook it, aware that Adam was watching them. "It's a pleasure to meet you, Mr. Golka."

Relief blossomed in his smile. "Trust Adam to have the most beautiful woman at the party. You always did have the best taste."

She flushed at his words, wondering if he was complimenting Adam's taste in women or his own. "Thank you."

"Look, I'd better get back to work," Lance said, tucking an empty tray under his arm. "But it was great to see you again, Adam. We'll have to get together sometime soon and share a few beers." His gaze drifted to Josie. "I need to fill you in on what I've been doing lately."

"Sounds good," Adam said, reaching into his jacket and pulling out a business card. "Just give me a call."

"I'll do that," Lance promised. Then he mouthed a silent thank-you to Josie as he turned and walked away.

She resumed her seat, still wondering if she'd made the right decision in keeping his secret. It wasn't as if she'd passed a point of no return. She could reveal Lance's identity as the impostor at any time. So why not give him an opportunity to make amends? To tell Adam the truth himself—perhaps even salvage their friendship.

"So, who was the stiff?" Woody asked.

"An old college roommate," Adam replied. "Lance Golka. He's the reason I'm here tonight."

"What do you mean?" Shondra queried. "Did the guy save your life or something?"

"Close." Adam picked up his wineglass. "He's the one who told me about the photography contest that led me to a career in outdoor photography. Otherwise, I'd be a lawyer right now."

"Not too much adventure in law," Shondra mused. "At least, I haven't seen too many lawyers hanging off bridges."

"Plenty of people who want to push lawyers off bridges, though," Ben said laughing.

His date wasn't amused. "My dad is a lawyer."

Ben cleared his throat. "It's a fine profession."

Josie didn't hear the rest of the conversation. She was too absorbed in trying to resolve the turmoil inside of her. How long should she keep Lance's secret? And why did she feel as if she were betraying Adam? The man didn't mean anything to her.

In fact, he'd been irritating her on a daily basis from the morning she'd awakened in his bed. He certainly didn't seem to have any problem manipulating her for his own purposes. The blackmail threat. The stolen shoes. His arrival at the book-club meeting this evening.

Now she had a chance to turn the tables on him. For the first time, Josie was the one in control. She smiled to herself, enjoying the sensation.

Then an announcement by the emcee broke her reverie. "And the Insanity Award goes to..." a drumroll sounded over the speakers, "Adam Delaney of *Adventurer* magazine."

Applause broke out among the crowd. Adam leaped to his feet, then impulsively leaned over to kiss her. It was over before she could react and, a moment later, she watched him walk toward the stage. Josie raised her fingers to her mouth, her lips still tingling. That brief contact had sent her heart rate soaring. Maybe she wasn't as much in control as she'd like to believe.

As she watched him give a short acceptance speech, Josie knew if she wasn't careful, she might make the mistake of falling for Adam. A risk worthy of the Insanity Award. A risk she wasn't willing to take.

"JUST ONE MORE FLIGHT," Adam said, walking up the fire stairs behind Josie.

"Did I mention I'm not fond of heights?" she asked, gripping the iron railing. The awards ceremony had ended fifteen minutes ago and the dancing had begun. Josie didn't like to dance and, to her surprise, neither did Adam. So he'd suggested taking her on an adventure instead. She should have refused, but she hadn't been thinking straight since that kiss.

"What floor are we on now?" she asked, slightly breathless from the steep climb.

"Twenty-five." He moved up beside her on the narrow stairs. "Only three more flights to go."

She kicked off her high heels, then trudged on despite her fatigue, not wanting to admit she couldn't make it. But, starting tomorrow, she was renewing her membership at the gym. "This had better be worth it."

"Oh, it will be," he promised, then took her hand in his own and helped her up the rest of the way.

At last, they reached the top of the stairs. Adam wrestled with the thick steel door a few moments, but finally wrenched it open. Then they stepped out onto the roof.

Josie looked at the panoramic view of Denver and her breath caught at the dazzling view. The city lights sparkled in the black-velvet night like a million stars. It was worth the climb.

"Like it?" he asked, moving beside her.

"It's incredible."

"So are you." Adam turned her in his arms. "I've been wanting to tell you that all evening."

His compliment made her feel even more guilty about keeping Lance's secret. Should she break her promise to him? Josie wasn't sure what to do, so she changed the subject. "Why do the fire stairs lead to the roof?"

He looked confused for a moment, then glanced back at the stairs. "I suppose in case a fire blocks all the exits on the lower floors. There's a helipad up here, so I'm guessing a helicopter rescue could be used."

She shivered, more from the thought of being trapped by a fire than the cool night breeze.

"Cold?" he asked, seeing her reaction.

She shook her head, but he took off his jacket anyway and draped it over her shoulders. It was still warm from his body, and she tugged the lapels more tightly around her, inhaling his unique scent. Wind ruffled his hair and she couldn't help but notice how magnificent he looked in the moonlight.

No matter how hard he tried, Lance Golka could never become Adam. And no matter how drawn she was to Adam, she could never become a permanent part of Adam's life. They moved in two different worlds. She couldn't delude herself as Lance had, no matter how much Adam tempted her.

Adam's hands rested lightly on her shoulders as they both enjoyed the view. She could feel the length of his body lightly pressing against her back.

"Thank you for coming here with me tonight." His warm breath spiraled into her ear, causing her entire body to tingle with awareness.

"To the roof?" she asked as his hands lightly massaged her shoulders. She swallowed a groan at the exquisite sensation. "Or to the awards ceremony?"

"Both."

"You're welcome." Now was the time to tell him the truth about Lance. Then they could go their separate ways. She wouldn't have to see him again. Wouldn't have to fight her own traitorous desires.

Turning around, she looked up at him, drawing in a deep breath. But he stopped her with a kiss and the words she needed to say came out as a hungry moan. Adam wrapped his arms around her waist, hauling her close against him.

His mouth moved feverishly on her lips while he kept her locked in his embrace, as if he feared she would try to escape. But escape was the last thing on Josie's mind. She writhed her body against his, telling herself this would be her last chance to kiss him. To touch him. The truth would come out and their reason for being together would end.

So she kissed him back with all the passion in her heart. Passion she'd kept locked away since that unforgettable night in his bed. She weaved her fingers through his thick hair and tugged him even closer, deepening the kiss.

Adam groaned low in his throat, his mouth gentling on her now. He raised his hands to her face, tenderly cupping her cheeks. Then he lifted his mouth long enough to whisper, "I want you, Jo. I need you."

His desire matched her own and Josie was mindless

with it. His hand caressed the curve of her buttocks, then lifted her until she straddled his waist, her dress riding up her thighs. He kissed her, moving until her back pressed against a brick chimney and Adam pressed into her.

His fingers glided along her inner thighs as his tongue explored her mouth. She whimpered softly as he rocked against her. Her fingers tugged the buttons open on his shirt, wanting to touch him as intimately as he touched her. She pulled his shirt open, splaying her hands on his warm, muscular chest. She smoothed them over his skin, across his flat nipples.

He tipped his head back, his eyes closed as her hands moved downward, fumbling with his belt. Then he grabbed her wrists and held them against the chimney, ravaging her with his mouth. First her lips, then her throat, then even lower.

She moaned softly as his tongue skimmed her collarbone, wanting more. So much more. He released one of her wrists to tug down the bodice, releasing her breasts. The cool night breeze pebbled her nipples, but he warmed them with his tongue. He swirled it expertly over one nipple, then the other, driving her to the brink with just his mouth.

Her body throbbed and she knew she couldn't take much more. With her free hand, she reached for the zipper of his slacks, knowing he was the only one who could quench the fire building inside of her. But something made her hesitate.

The sound of voices on the stairs finally penetrated through the haze of their desire. They broke apart, their breathing heavy and haggard as they hastily adjusted their clothing.

Josie tugged up the bodice of her dress, horrified by what had almost happened. There was no doubt in her mind that they'd been only moments away from making love on the roof. Where anyone could have seen them.

This was just further proof that she couldn't trust herself with Adam. His power over her was too great. Too seductive. Too dangerous.

The door to the fire stairs opened and two couples walked out. They glanced at Adam and Josie, then giggled as they moved to the other side of the roof.

"I think we should find someplace a little more private," he whispered, slipping one arm around her waist. "The sooner, the better."

Lance Golka had never evoked this kind of response in her. Neither had any other man. But was it simply lust or something more? There was only one way to find out.

She wanted Adam so desperately it terrified her. She'd seen what that kind of desperation could do to people. Seen how it could ultimately destroy.

Go for it, her heart told her. *Take the risk.* But her head weighed the consequences. A man like Adam wasn't into commitments. Hadn't he made that clear this evening, telling her that his job was his life?

Josie knew she couldn't give him her body without giving him her heart as well. A heart he hadn't asked for and probably didn't want. Which meant she'd be following the same disastrous path as her parents. Letting passion lead the way instead of logic.

"I think I should call a cab," Josie said, before she had a chance to change her mind.

He frowned, his thumb caressing the curve of her cheek. "What's the matter?"

His tender touch almost undid her. She pulled away. "I need to go home."

Then she turned and headed toward the stairs before he could change her mind.

But Adam was beside her in an instant, grabbing her arm to stop her. "Josie, wait. I can take you home—if that's what you really want."

She looked into his eyes, hoping he couldn't see what she really wanted. Knowing her fragile willpower would crumble if he as much as kissed her again. "I'd rather take a cab. I never should have come here this evening. That was a mistake. A big mistake."

"The way you kissed me just now was no mistake." His fingers curled around her wrist. "You can't just walk away."

She swallowed hard, searching for the words that would make him let her go. Even if she had to lie. "I shouldn't be kissing anyone, Adam. I already have a boyfriend."

He blanched, then released her as if she'd burned

him. She spun around and hurried through the door leading to the fire stairs. Taking the steps two at a time, she catapulted down the stairs, sliding along the railing to keep her balance. But she didn't need to hurry; Adam hadn't followed her.

When she finally reached the front sidewalk and hailed a taxi, Josie realized she wasn't wearing her shoes. They were still on the twenty-fifth floor, where she'd kicked them off on the way up to the roof.

As the cab pulled up to the curb, she debated whether to go back for them. They weren't cheap, but no expense was worth running into Adam again, not when she remembered the look on his face when she'd mentioned her boyfriend.

"Forget the shoes," she muttered to herself, climbing into the backseat of the cab. "Forget Adam. Forget everything."

10

THE NEXT DAY, everyone on staff at *Adventurer* magazine soon learned to stay out of Adam's way. Everyone except Woody. He was disgustingly cheerful, even in the face of Adam's foul mood.

"I'm in love," Woody said, waltzing into Adam's office. "Look, isn't she gorgeous?"

Adam glanced up from the dismantled camera on his desk to see a fuzzy picture of a woman, still fresh from the color printer. "It's hard to tell."

"She is gorgeous," Woody persisted, gazing at the picture. "And smart and funny and crazy about me."

"Or maybe just crazy," Adam muttered, carefully wiping a wide-angle lens. "How do you even know that's really a picture of her?"

"I don't," Woody admitted with a grin. "But I soon will. We have a date tomorrow night."

Adam looked up at him. "She lives in Denver?"

"Scottsbluff, Nebraska," Woody informed him. "She's a nurse at the hospital there, but she's taking the weekend off to drive here and meet me."

"Well, good luck," Adam said wryly. He'd be spending the weekend with Horatio. His cat was the only company he could stand at the moment. At least Horatio didn't go on and on about Josie. So far this morning, he'd heard Ben, the intern and even Shondra gush about how much they liked her now that they'd gotten to know her better.

Adam, on the other hand, doubted he'd ever really know her. Or know what she was thinking. Last night on the roof, he'd been foolish enough to believe that they'd finally connected—emotionally as well as physically. That he'd finally broken through the protective wall she'd erected around herself. He'd glimpsed that wild woman once more in that kiss. He'd been ready to declare victory until she'd brought up the subject of her boyfriend. Her *impostor* boyfriend.

What the hell was wrong with her? With him? Why was he wasting his morning dwelling on a woman who was devoted to the man trying to ruin his life?

Because I'm falling in love with her.

The answer came unbidden to his mind and he quickly shoved it out again. Adam Delaney didn't fall in love. He didn't have time. His only love was his work. He enjoyed the company of women, but his passion was photography. The search for the perfect shot. He simply didn't have room in his life for anything or anyone else.

"Earth to Adam."

He looked up to find Woody standing on the other side of his desk. "Oh, are you still here?"

"I've been here for the last five minutes. Where have you been?" Woody held up both hands, a goofy grin on his face. "No, let me take a guess. You've been wandering around on the planet Josie."

"Wrong," Adam retorted, turning his attention back to cleaning his camera.

"I think I'm right," Woody countered, perching himself on one corner of the desk. "That would explain your bad mood this morning. In fact, now that I think about it, you weren't too happy last night, either. When I left the ballroom, you were at the bar, holding a whiskey in one hand and Josie's shoes in the other. So what happened to the rest of her?"

"She went home."

"Home?" Woody's brow crinkled. "Alone? And without her shoes?"

"Don't ask me to explain women," he replied, wishing he'd foregone that whiskey last night. A dull headache throbbed in his temple.

"But you're the expert." Woody gazed at the picture in his hand once more, then turned his attention back to Adam. "That's why I come to you for all my romantic advice."

"Yeah, I'm a real expert." He wondered once again what had happened last night. One minute Josie had been kissing him senseless, the next she'd been running for the door. Unless he'd completely misread that kiss. No, not possible. Not with her hands on his zipper.

Woody laughed. "You may be an expert on women, but I'm the expert on love and you've got all the classic symptoms."

Adam snorted. "Have you been sampling those hallucinogens again? Because you're in dreamland."

"Am I?" Woody challenged. "I've never seen you in a mood like this before. Heck, I've never seen you look at a woman the way you were looking at Josie last night. You haven't been drinking much lately either—until she left you like Cinderella at the ball."

He fingered the polishing cloth on his desk, the soft fabric reminding him of her flawless skin. "A mistake I intend to rectify. I'm going to the Alligator Bar tonight. Want to come along?"

Woody ignored the invitation. "Another classic symptom—drowning your sorrows. Tell me something, Adam. Do you find yourself thinking about her all the time? Dwelling on everything she's said and what you said and what it all meant? Do little things constantly remind you of her?"

"Not at all," he lied, dropping the polishing cloth onto the desk.

Woody shrugged his thin shoulders. "I guess it's possible I could be wrong."

"Dead wrong," Adam assured him, though now he knew he was lying to himself as well as Woody. Everything the man said was true. He was falling for Josie. He'd known it last night when she'd brought up her boyfriend. Jealousy, hot and swift, rose in him once again, just as it had last night.

So why was he so resistant to the idea of falling in love with her? Adam had never backed down from a challenge before. A relationship with Josie might be the biggest adventure of all. She was never predictable. Never boring, either. They were polar opposites, but he felt more fire with her than with any woman he'd ever known.

Now he just had to find a way to convince her they belonged together. As well as figure out a way to get her impostor boyfriend out of the picture, once and for all.

"Well, it's been a trip," Woody said, hopping off the desk and heading toward the door. "But I suppose I'd better get back to work before Ben blows his toupee."

Adam needed to get to work, too. He'd been going about this all wrong, trying to strong-arm Josie into helping him find the impostor when he should have been finding ways to win her over to his side. Last night, he'd thought seducing her was the answer, but he'd failed.

It was time to change his strategy.

BY MONDAY MORNING, Josie still wasn't convinced she'd made the right decision about concealing Lance's identity from Adam. She didn't regret leaving him on the rooftop, though. She'd lost her head that night, caught up in the romance of a sexy interlude under the stars.

Now, in the light of day, she realized it had been an illusion. The only reason Adam had wanted her with him was to identify his impostor. That kiss had meant nothing special to him. Being a man, he wasn't about to turn away a willing woman. The night she'd spent in his bed had proven that.

Josie had lost her shoes, but she'd kept her heart. She'd passed the danger point, vanquishing the battle of her desire for him. She felt stronger now. Safer. She'd resisted Adam's charms and the dangerous pull of her own passion.

She turned her attention to her work, losing herself in research on the ancient Mayans. Until the aroma of jasmine filled her nostrils. Looking up, she saw a delivery man in front of her desk holding a potted plant.

"Josephine Sinclair?" he inquired.

She put down her pen. "Yes?"

"This is for you." He set the pot on an empty corner of her desk, then plucked the card from the plant and handed it to her. "Have a nice day."

"Thank you," she murmured automatically, her gaze falling to the bold, black print on the card. But she waited until the delivery man had left before she read it.

Jo
The scent of jasmine will always remind me of you. Thank you for helping me search for the im-

postor. All I ask is one more adventure together—
a trip to my hometown of Pleasant Valley, Colorado, for the annual town picnic. If my impostor
isn't there, I'll be ready to move on with my life.
Please say you'll come.

Adam

Josie read the card again, gently tracing her finger
over his name. She was twenty-seven years old and no
man had ever sent her flowers before, much less something exotic like jasmine.

His thoughtfulness touched her, even as she realized that Lance must not have made his confession
yet. She knew Adam wouldn't find his impostor at
Pleasant Valley's annual town picnic. Still, it might be
fun to go with him. One last flirtation with her wild
side before she settled back into her comfortable life.

"What am I thinking?" Josie scolded herself, placing the card in her desk. Then she picked up the telephone with every intention of turning down his invitation.

He answered on the first ring and the sound of his
voice made her waver. "Jo?"

"How did you know it was me?"

"I have caller I.D. It shows the Denver Public Library, so I made a wild guess."

She smiled. "Thank you for the jasmine plant. It's
lovely."

"You're welcome."

Twisting the phone cord in her fingers, she said, "About this weekend..."

"I think it will be a lot of fun," Adam interjected. "Good food and good people. It's a little hokey, but that's part of the charm."

She hesitated, wondering if she should risk it. Then again, what better way to prove her immunity to him? That might be the only way she could put him behind her. And if Lance hadn't confessed his role as Adam's impostor by then, she could finally tell him the truth. Then he truly could move on with his life.

And so could she.

"It sounds like a wonderful time," Josie said at last. "Count me in."

"Great," he exclaimed. "I'll pick you up at your place about ten o'clock on Saturday morning. That should get us there in time for lunch."

She didn't want to hang up, but there wasn't anything left to say. "I'll see you then."

"I'm looking forward to it, Jo."

Placing the receiver back on the cradle, she was surprised to find her palms damp with perspiration. Accepting an invitation to a picnic wasn't as risky as hanging off a bridge, but a sense of danger seemed to permeate the very air she breathed. Resisting Adam once had been difficult enough. Resisting him twice might prove impossible.

Not that he'd hinted at romance during the telephone call. In fact, their conversation had been free of the sexual innuendos she'd come to expect from him. Perhaps he'd finally given up. Or found someone else to occupy his attention.

That thought gave her pause. He only asked her places to identify his impostor. That was the only reason he'd invited her to lunch at Spagli's, the company party, the awards ceremony at The Pines and now the Pleasant Valley town picnic. She was simply reading too much into this invitation, jasmine or no jasmine.

The head librarian walked by her desk, pausing to admire her jasmine plant. "Where did you find this beautiful plant?"

"A friend sent it to me," Josie hedged.

The director arched an eyebrow. "Well, I must say he has lovely taste. It is a he, isn't it?"

"Yes," Josie admitted. "His name is Adam. Adam Delaney."

"Adam Delaney," she repeated, her brow furrowed. "That name certainly sounds familiar. Is he a regular patron?"

"No, Adam is a photographer for *Adventurer* magazine."

The librarian nodded. "That's where I've seen the name before. We have several issues of *Adventurer* magazine in our archives." Then her eyes narrowed. "Is this the same man who was here shouting at you last week?"

"He wasn't exactly shouting, but yes, that was Adam."

"Hmm." Evelyn plucked a withered leaf off the base of the plant. "I see he's trying to redeem himself. Well, this is certainly a good start. He just received some kind of award, didn't he? I believe I read something about it in the newspaper over the weekend."

"It was the Insanity Award," she said, a quiver of pride in her voice, "given for taking the riskiest photograph."

The librarian shuddered. "I've seen some of those pictures in *Adventurer* magazine. The last issue featured his foray into some Central American jungle. It's a wonder the man is still alive."

Josie didn't want to think about the risks Adam took with his life. Once he knew that Lance Golka was his impostor, he'd be off on another dangerous adventure. She nibbled her lower lip, faced with a dilemma. Maybe it would be better if he never knew, especially if that was the only way she could keep him safe.

"Is something wrong?" Evelyn asked. "You look worried."

Josie shook herself out of her reverie. "No, I'm perfectly fine. I was just wondering if it might be possible to rearrange the work schedule. I'm down for Saturday, but something has come up."

Evelyn thought about it for a moment. "I don't think that will be a problem, as long as you're willing to work another Saturday."

"Of course," Josie agreed. "Thank you, Evelyn. I appreciate it."

Her boss leaned down to sniff the jasmine, closing her eyes briefly at the heavenly scent. "You might want to do a little research on the proper care of a jasmine plant. Colorado is definitely not its natural environment."

She nodded. "I'll do that."

The director started to walk away, then hesitated before turning back to Josie. "I know your personal life is your own business, but…"

"Yes?" Josie queried, having never seen the efficient Evelyn at a loss for words before.

She drew up her shoulders. "But the world of people like Adam Delaney isn't the natural environment of librarians, either. Please be careful."

Josie nodded, taking the older woman's warning to heart. "I always am."

11

JOSIE'S EXPECTATIONS of spending an idyllic Saturday afternoon on a picnic with Adam were dashed when he picked her up that morning.

"I think I've nailed him," Adam said the moment they set off for Pleasant Valley in his Camaro.

"Nailed who?"

"My impostor." He raced through a yellow light at an intersection, then turned onto a highway, heading south out of Denver.

Josie's first thought was that he knew about Lance. But, if that was the case, why did he want to take her to Pleasant Valley? And wouldn't he be asking her why she hadn't exposed Lance at the awards ceremony?

But instead of hurling accusations, he gave her a slow, sexy smile, his gaze taking in the strapless red sundress she wore. "You look wonderful."

"Thank you," she said, smoothing the skirt over her knees. She'd found it in the back of her closet this morning, a dress she'd bought on impulse two years ago, but had never worn.

His compliment and the heat in his eyes unsettled

her, so she changed the subject. "Who do you suspect is your impostor?"

Adam sighed, resting his wrist atop the steering wheel. "His name is Carter Haywood. I grew up with the guy in Pleasant Valley. In fact, he lived right down the gravel road from our house."

Josie heaved an inner sigh of relief. Lance's secret was still safe—and so was her part in it. "Why would this Carter Haywood want to take over your life?"

Adam shrugged. "Payback, I guess. We were rivals in high school. All because he thought I'd stolen his girl."

"Did you?"

"No, but Carter will never see it that way. He'd been in love with Lisa Dugan since junior high. I knew it, so when she came on to me the summer after we graduated, I turned her down as gently as I could. But Lisa didn't take rejection well. So she struck back by telling Haywood that I had made a move on her."

"And he believed her?"

Adam's gaze stayed on the long ribbon of highway stretched out in front of them. "Love can make people crazy sometimes."

Given her family's past, Josie couldn't argue with him. Even now, she wondered about her own sanity. Like telling herself this picnic would be a good test of her immunity to him. Now she knew it was just an excuse to see him again.

"Wait a minute," she said still trying to make sense

of his suspicion, "that happened how many years ago?"

"It's been almost twelve years."

"*Twelve years?*" She shook her head. "No one would hold a grudge that long. Carter Haywood is not the impostor."

"It might be twelve years to you and me, but it's still fresh in Carter's mind. He brought the subject up again at our high school reunion last summer, even throwing a punch at me. Sure, we'd both had a few beers, but even drunk he vowed to get back at me someday."

Josie swallowed, knowing another fight could break out if Adam accused this man of impersonating him. At least she could prevent that from happening. "I'll take a good look at him and let you know if he's the one."

Adam shook his head. "See, that's the problem. Carter runs a big ranch outfit now. He couldn't be gone for months at a time. But he does have enough money to hire somebody to do the job."

"You really believe he'd go to that extreme to get revenge? After all, it was just a silly high school crush."

He glanced at her. "Do you think I *want* it to be Carter? The thought makes me sick to my stomach. We've had a few rocky times, but he's basically a decent guy. The problem is that I can't come up with anybody else who holds any kind of grudge against me."

Josie thought of Lance, knowing his grudge was more against himself for not following his dreams.

"Believe me," Adam continued, "I've laid awake nights trying to figure it out. Carter is the only one who even comes close to fitting that description."

"But you don't know for sure," she reminded him. "Maybe you should just let it go."

"No way." His jaw tightened. "I need to know the truth. I need to know if he betrayed me."

"And then what?" she asked softly.

"Then I'll know I can never trust him again. But at least my life will be my own again."

They approached a long strip of highway construction. Orange signs dotted the shoulder of the road, warning drivers of a lane closed ahead.

"Damn," Adam said, applying the brakes to the Camaro. "I should have taken the other route. I told my father we'd be there by noon."

"Did you tell your family about the impostor? Do they know that's the reason I'm coming to the picnic with you?"

He shook his head. "I didn't want to worry them."

"Then how will you explain me?"

He flashed her a smile. "Simple. You're my date for the picnic."

Josie wished it was that simple. But her promise to keep Lance's secret was only making her life more complicated. She couldn't let Adam confront Carter

Haywood, given their history. But how could she stop him without revealing the truth?

Maybe by revealing a piece of her own past.

"It's nice you're close to your family," she began, turning her gaze to the window. "I haven't seen my father for over five years."

Adam kept the car moving at a snail's pace, vehicles backed up on the one-lane highway for almost a mile "Why so long?"

"Because he's never really forgiven me for sending him to jail."

He slammed on the brakes, after almost hitting the car in front of him. Then he turned to stare at her. "You sent your father to jail?"

"Not on purpose," she clarified. Josie had never told this story to anyone, not even Lance. It was simply too painful, a part of the past that she'd rather forget. But if it kept Adam from accusing the wrong man, then it was simply the price she had to pay.

"My parents divorced when I was twelve years old," Josie explained, "after my mother fell in love with another man. She got full custody of me, and my father was allowed visits every other weekend. Only, on one of those weekends, he didn't take me back. We were gone for over a month."

"He abducted you?"

She nodded. "It wasn't...malicious. He was desperate to find some way to reach my mother. He was still in love with her and wanted us back together as a family. I did, too. Only I didn't realize what he was doing was illegal."

Adam gave her his full attention. "So what happened?"

The story was harder to tell than she'd imagined, even though it had happened over fifteen years ago. "I called my mother from a motel room in St. Louis, just to let her know I was all right and that Dad had promised to take me home soon. I didn't know that the police had placed a tracer on my mother's telephone. My phone call led to his arrest."

Adam's brow furrowed. "You were only twelve. How could you know?"

She wouldn't let him make excuses for her. "That didn't matter to my father. He still thought I'd betrayed him. That I'd chosen sides."

"Damn." He gripped his hands around the steering wheel. "Some parents just don't get it."

"Mine didn't," Josie said softly. "They were too caught up in their battle to notice what it was doing to me—or to care. They just let their emotions take control of them."

He turned to look at her and for a moment Josie thought he was going to pull her into his arms and console her. When he didn't, she took a deep breath and told herself she was becoming maudlin. "It was all a long time ago."

"You don't have to be tough with me, you know," Adam replied. "I won't hurt you."

If only she could believe him. But Josie knew how easily this man could destroy her. How vulnerable she was to him even now.

"But your accusation might hurt other people," she said, her voice tight. "Your parents live in this town. I assume they see Carter from time to time."

Adam nodded, looking both thoughtful and frustrated. "I guess I don't have any real proof."

She breathed a sigh of relief. "When you find your impostor, and I believe you will before long, you might be surprised to discover that his reason for impersonating you wasn't malicious. He might have a reasonable explanation for his actions."

"There you go defending him again," Adam said wryly. "Tell me what's reasonable about masquerading as another man for three months? Using my name, my apartment and my credentials to serve himself."

Josie felt as if she was on solid ground once more. She took a deep breath. Debate she could handle. It was emotions that gave her problems.

"Maybe his actions wouldn't be reasonable to you or me," she conceded, "but that doesn't necessarily make him evil. Look at my father. Yes, he abducted me. Yes, my mother suffered because of it. Only she didn't seem to realize that my father was suffering, too. Otherwise, he never would have done something so desperate."

"So you're saying my impostor must have been desperate for some reason?"

"I don't know." Josie didn't want to start analyzing Lance's behavior. She still didn't understand why he hadn't confessed to Adam yet. Maybe he hadn't worked up enough courage. Should she give him a few more days before she broke her promise to keep his secret?

If she could convince Adam not to accuse Carter Haywood, she would wait.

"All I know," she continued, "is that my mother was more interested in revenge than reconciliation. She pushed the district attorney to press full charges against my father."

"And he blamed you?"

She nodded, tears welling in her throat. A ridiculous reaction, since this had happened over fifteen years ago. But something about Adam seemed to bring all her emotions to the surface.

"That wasn't fair," Adam said, anger reverberating in his voice. "What happened between your parents is not your fault."

"Maybe not." She swallowed hard, refusing to cry in front of him. "My father never came right out and said it, but I know I hurt him deeply. I could see the disappointment in his face when he thought I'd chosen my mother over him. Our relationship has never been the same again."

Adam reached out and touched her hand. "That's his loss."

Josie's breath caught in her throat as she turned her

gaze back to him. He leaned closer to her, his broad fingers curling around her hand. Awareness prickled over her body as his gaze fell to her mouth. She closed her eyes, waiting for his kiss. Anticipating it with every beat of her heart.

But the blast of a horn behind them shattered the moment. Adam let go of her hand and shifted the Camaro into gear as the long line of cars ahead of them began to slowly move forward.

It took Josie longer to make the transition. When she could think again, she remembered Adam's words. *That's his loss.* The words echoed in her head and warmed her heart. For so many years, Josie had wallowed in guilt for unwittingly betraying her father. Adam had only said what she'd told herself often enough. But somehow, hearing it from him made all the difference in the world.

Which made Adam more dangerous than ever.

ADAM LAY ON A BLANKET, looking up at foothills framed by the bright azure sky and wondered when he'd ever been this content. Josie sat beside him, finishing the last bite of carrot cake in her hand.

"I can't believe you baked this," she said, licking the spicy crumbs off of her fingers.

"You've now sampled the extent of my culinary talent—frittatas and carrot cake."

The meadow was dotted with blankets, the people of Pleasant Valley having turned out in full force for the annual town picnic. Adam had contributed the food he'd brought with him to the potluck table, pointing out his dishes to Josie. She'd skipped the buffalo jerky and the deli potato salad, but had indulged in two pieces of carrot cake.

Now she groaned as she stretched out beside him, propping her head up on one hand. "I'm completely stuffed."

"Then you'll be glad to know that the annual town picnic is followed by the annual town nap."

She laughed softly, looking at all the people dozing around them. "It looks very tempting."

He turned to face her, wondering if she knew how beautiful she was at this moment. "So do you."

Sunlight cast golden streaks in her blond hair, all bound up in her neat bun. On impulse, he reached up and loosened it, pulling all the bobby pins from her hair.

"Hey," she protested, trying to stop the cascade of curls that came tumbling down around her face.

He flashed a teasing smile. "Didn't I tell you that hair accessories of any kind are forbidden at public events in Pleasant Valley? All due to a tragic event with a metal headband. The mayor stepped on it at the last picnic and almost lost his big toe."

"And you expect me to buy that?"

He nodded. "It's a town ordinance passed just last year. You can check it out with my dad if you don't believe me."

Josie glanced over at his parents' blanket. "It looks like they're napping."

"Either that or making out. I try not to look, just in case."

She leaned back on her elbows. "Well, if there really is a law against hair accessories, I'm surprised the sheriff hasn't hauled me off to jail." She nodded toward the officer dozing just a few yards away from them.

"He probably let you off because you're with me," Adam informed her. "I carry a lot of weight in this town."

"The last thing I want to do is break the law." She removed the thick elastic band that had also been securing her hair and fluffed it out with her fingers. Then she lay back on the blanket, staring up at the sky. "By the way, you'll be carrying a lot of weight in Denver, too, if you keep eating like that. Did you have four pieces of fried chicken or five?"

"Six," he confessed. "My mom's fried chicken is one of my weaknesses."

"And here I thought you were perfect. Tell me some of your other weaknesses."

"Lemon-meringue pie," he began, looking down at her and inhaling the scent of jasmine. It was the same perfume she'd worn on the night they'd made love and it evoked memories that made his body tighten with desire. "Big green eyes. Stern librarians."

She met his gaze with a frown. "You're teasing me again."

"Am I?" he whispered, leaning closer. Only a few more inches and he could kiss that luscious mouth, knowing she'd taste of cinnamon and frosting and her own unique flavor. But he pulled back, just as he'd done in the car, reminding himself to be on his best behavior today. He wanted to romance her. To convince her that he was interested in more than sex.

Now he just had to convince his throbbing body.

"How would you like to see my biggest weakness?" Adam asked her, ready to put his plan into action.

"Hmm," she murmured sleepily, "that sounds intriguing. Where do I have to look?"

He sat up and held out his hand. "Come with me and I'll show you."

She hesitated a moment, then let him pull her to her feet before she dropped his hand. "Shall we tell your parents we're leaving?"

Adam looked over by the towering pine where his parents had laid their blanket. His father lay snuggled next to his mother. "I don't think they'll miss us."

She followed him up a dirt path, away from the rest of the picnickers. "Where are we going?"

"You'll see," he promised, lifting a branch out of her way and letting her pass ahead of him.

He took her hand again and she didn't pull away. *Progress*, he told himself, then smiled inwardly at the irony of it. He'd made love to this woman before he'd even known her name and now he was thrilled when she let him hold her hand.

They walked along the path, moving farther into the rocky wilderness of the foothills. Snow capped the tall peaks of the mountains, but the weather was warm along the winding dirt trail.

"How much farther is this weakness of yours?" Josie asked, sounding a little breathless.

It was a hard climb, even for someone like Adam who had grown up in the area. "We're almost there."

At last they came to a plateau, high enough that the colorful blankets spread out in the meadow below looked like tiny square tiles. Josie sat down on a flat boulder to catch her breath and enjoy the view. "I don't think I can climb any higher."

"You don't have to," he announced. "We're here."

She looked around at the pine trees and assorted boulders. "This is it?"

He pointed to the gap in the outcropping of rock in front of her. "Right there. I call it Delaney's Cave. It was my secret hideaway while I was growing up. You're one of the few people who even know it exists."

She blanched. "A cave? As in dark, narrow and claustrophobic?"

He laughed. "I guess that's in the eye of the beholder. I think of it as snug, cozy and private. Would you like to take a look?"

"I'm not sure," she said warily. "It's probably a very nice cave, but..."

He smiled at the expression on her face. "But you're not a fan of caves?"

"I've never actually been in one," she admitted. "And I'm not sure I want to start now."

"Where's your adventurous spirit?"

She arched an eyebrow. "I think you're talking to the wrong girl."

He held out his hand. "I dare you."

Josie knew she shouldn't take the bait, but something in his tone made her rise to her feet. "All right, I'll do it."

He led her toward the narrow opening in the rock, knowing he should probably warn her that they might not be the only occupants. "Watch out for the snakes."

"Snakes?" Josie stopped abruptly, causing Adam to run into her. He grasped her waist to keep her from pitching forward, his fingers plunging into the soft curve of her hips.

"Small snakes," he replied, letting his hands linger on her. "Completely harmless."

"But you're saying there *could* be snakes in there, right? I mean, it's not beyond the realm of possibility."

He wanted to kick himself for opening his big mouth. "Yes, but the good news is, if we go in, they'll go out. Snakes aren't as fond of humans as we are of them."

She turned around. "The last thing I want to do is evict a snake from a snug, cozy cave."

Adam stood directly in front of her, his hands still on her waist. He tugged her closer, her lips parting as her eyes met his.

Once again, Josie sensed that he wanted to kiss her. All he had to do was lean forward, tilt his head just a little, touch his mouth to hers...

The fantasy ended when Adam dropped his hands from her and stepped around her to enter the cave. "I'll go on ahead and check it out," he said. "If the cave is snake-free, I'll give the all clear signal."

Josie watched him disappear into the cave, wondering what was wrong with him, why he hadn't kissed her. Or was she expecting too much? Flirtation came as naturally to Adam as breathing. It didn't mean anything to him. *She* didn't mean anything to him.

Plopping back down on the rock, she was tired from the climb and disgusted with her own delusions. Adam had only asked her to the picnic to identify his impostor. Fortunately, he'd decided not to confront Carter Haywood, especially when he discovered the man was engaged to be married and deliriously in love.

So, in Adam's eyes, her usefulness had ended, but obviously he was too polite to ignore her. And too much of a gentleman to lead her on.

The possibility that Adam could see the desire for him that she'd tried so desperately to hide made Josie feel a little sick to her stomach. He could have any woman he wanted and he'd made it quite clear today that he didn't want her.

Josie brushed the hair off her face, wishing she hadn't left the elastic band on the blanket. Wishing she'd never come here today.

Several minutes later, Adam emerged from the cave. Dust speckled his face and he wiped his hands on his jeans. "The cave is snake-free and ready for a full tour."

"I think I'll skip the tour," she said coolly. It was time she stopped fantasizing about Adam. "In fact, I'd like you to take me home. I'm not feeling well."

His brow furrowed. "What's wrong?"

She shook her head, not about to tell him the real reason. "I'm not sure. It might have been something I ate. Can we please just go?"

"Of course." He reached for her hand, but she turned quickly onto the path, pretending not to see it.

All the way back to the meadow, she chided herself for reading more into Adam's actions than were really there. He'd held her hand to help her up the steep path. He'd probably pulled the bun from her hair just to annoy her. With each step, she convinced herself that she'd been reading too much into his words and actions. That her own unruly passion for him had clouded her thinking.

A mistake she wouldn't let happen again.

When they reached the meadow, Adam gathered

the blanket and picnic basket while Josie politely bid his parents goodbye. They were nice people, whichfor some irrational reason made her even more upset.

When they reached the Camaro, Adam stowed the picnic basket and the blanket in the trunk while Josie climbed into the passenger seat. She refrained from slamming the door, but the anger kept building inside of her. Anger at Adam for forcing her into his life. Anger at herself for wanting so much to be a part of it.

When he slid behind the steering wheel, she turned to face him. "I'm sorry we didn't find your impostor today. I'm sure you will find him soon, but I can't help you anymore."

Adam started the engine. "Maybe we should talk about this later, when you're feeling better."

"Fine," she agreed, closing her eyes and leaning against the headrest to keep him from making conversation. But she knew they wouldn't be talking about it later, because she had no intention of ever seeing Adam Delaney again.

12

JOSIE PAUSED AT THE ENTRANCE to the library's meeting room, unable to believe her eyes. Adam Delaney sat among the circle of book-club members, a copy of *Wuthering Heights* in his lap. She hadn't even considered the possibility that he'd show up there again.

It had been five days since their trip to Pleasant Valley. He'd called her several times since then, but she'd avoided picking up the telephone and hadn't returned any of his messages. Josie had assumed he'd get the hint, but obviously she'd been wrong. The question was what to do now? Skip out on the meeting or face him head-on?

Squaring her shoulders, Josie stepped inside the meeting room, refusing to run away. She had told Adam on Saturday that she didn't intend to help him hunt for his impostor anymore. She didn't need to feel guilty about keeping his impostor's identity a secret, either. Lance had stopped by the library yesterday, giving her his new address and assuring her that he planned to tell everything to Adam this weekend. He'd already saved up some money to repay him for some of the photography supplies that he'd used in Adam's darkroom.

Fully contrite, Lance had even hinted at resuming a relationship with her. But Josie had gently intimated that their relationship was over. She needed a braver man than Lance in her life. A man not afraid to take a few risks. A man like Adam.

Too bad he didn't want her.

She avoided Adam's gaze as she took her seat. "Good evening. I'm so glad to see everyone here tonight."

"I almost didn't come," the pregnant homemaker confided. "This book was so depressing."

"*Wuthering Heights* is a classic gothic novel," Josie replied, wondering if Adam had read this book as well. It definitely had some lessons that he needed to learn. "Cathy and Heathcliff show us how the clash of strong passions can ultimately destroy people."

"That's because they were idiots," Adam commented.

She blinked, taken aback by his frankness. "Idiots?"

He nodded. "Look, they were in love. But instead of trying to find a solution to their problems, they each just made things worse."

"It was a different time," Tina the hairdresser said. "A different society. Just look at how Brontë displayed the vast differences between the classes."

"I'm not sure it's so different today," the dental hygienist said with a sigh. "Love seems as complicated as ever."

Adam's gaze centered on Josie. "It doesn't have to be complicated. Unless you're afraid of your own feelings. Like...Cathy."

"Heathcliff was the problem," Josie countered. "He made her life miserable."

"Only because she kept running away from him," Adam replied.

"They both died," Helen said. "Their passion for each other destroyed them."

"That's what can happen when you lose control," Josie told the group, her pulse racing in spite of herself. "Too many people lead with their heart instead of their head."

"Now *that* is depressing," the pregnant Nancy said. "Love isn't supposed to be neat and tidy. It can be messy and unpredictable and wonderful all at the same time." She smiled as she rested her hand on her protruding stomach. "And it can lead to unexpected developments along the way."

"Some people don't like unexpected developments," Adam said. "They like to plan out everything to the last detail. And when those plans change, they panic. Right, Jo?"

She met his gaze and knew he was referring to that night in his bed. He wanted her to admit that she had panicked. And that the unexpected development in her life was falling in love with him. Both were true.

"Never mind," Adam said at last. He stood up, tucking the book under his arm. "Maybe I read it all wrong."

"You're leaving?" The hygienist blinked up at him in surprise. "But we're just getting started with the discussion. And you have so many interesting things to say. We all think it's fascinating to hear about romance from a man's perspective."

A muscle flexed in his jaw. "Not all of you." Then he turned and stalked out the door.

Josie stared after him, torn between running after him and locking the door behind him. Inside, she felt as cold and desolate as the moors in *Wuthering Heights*. Outside, she forced a smile and tried to pretend everything was all right. "So, what did everyone think about Lockwood?"

"Are you completely crazy?" Helen asked her. "You just let a man like that walk out of here without saying one word to stop him?"

"It's not that simple," Josie replied. "We're not... compatible."

"Oh, please," Tina said with a wave of her hand. "My husband and I are so compatible that he's asleep on the sofa before eight o'clock every night. In my book, compatible is just another word for predictable."

Josie didn't know how to respond, so she tried to salvage the book discussion. "Thrushcross Grange provided an interesting contrast to Wuthering Heights. How do you think it reflected the theme of the story?"

"I have absolutely no idea," Giselle said, "but the theme of my life seems to be that a good man isn't hard to find, he's impossible to find. Adam Delaney strikes me as a very good man. So, honey, if you don't want him, I'll be more than happy to take him off your hands."

"I never said I didn't want him," Josie retorted. "I'm just not so sure he wants me. Not permanently, anyway."

"He sure acts like he wants you," Tina said wistfully. "Like bringing you that beautiful dress a week ago."

"And joining our book club," Nancy added. "Just look around. How many men do you see here? He even made it all the way through Wuthering Heights. Now that's what I call true devotion."

"Me, too," Helen agreed. "Anybody could see just by looking at him that the guy's crazy about you."

They all made it sound so simple. As if she could just follow her heart and damn the consequences. Just like her mother had. Yet, who was happier? Her mother, who had followed her heart into an uncertain future? Or her father, who had tried too hard to cling to the security of the past and had paid the price for it?

Josie sat back in her chair, stunned by the realization that by avoiding the pain she'd experienced in the past she was avoiding love. Lance Golka had been safe because she'd never been in danger of loving him. Not like Adam, who had touched not only her body the night they'd made love, but her heart and her soul.

That's why she'd been running from him ever since.

Nancy was right. Love *was* messy and unpredictable. It offered no guarantees. No safety nets along the way. Hearts could break. Marriages and families and dreams could all be shattered if love went wrong, as it had for her parents.

But what if love went right?

Josie had been too worried about the dangers of falling in love to realize the dangers of *not* falling in love. Days filled with loneliness. A life full of regrets. Dreams that could never come true.

It all seemed so obvious to her now. Why hadn't she seen that denying her love for Adam wouldn't save her from heartache?

In fact, just the opposite. It practically guaranteed it.

"I love him," she said aloud, wanting to shout it from the rooftops. If only she'd stayed on that roof at The Pines instead of running away that night, she might have come to this revelation even sooner. "I am in love with Adam Delaney."

"Well, don't tell us," Helen said with a smile. "Go tell *him*."

"I will," Josie announced, feeling giddy and nervous and scared. But that was all right. It was better than feeling nothing at all.

"This is the best meeting we've ever had," Tina said. "I can't wait until next week."

"I'm crazy about Dickens," Nancy said. "Shall we try something by him, like *Great Expectations?*"

Josie nodded. "And how about *Robinson Crusoe* the week after that? I'm ready to add some adventure to my life."

They all enthusiastically agreed. After weeks of trying to get her book-club members to talk, now Josie couldn't get them to stop talking so she could close the library and go find Adam.

Twenty minutes later, she got them all out the door, locking it from the inside. She grabbed her purse, her quick footsteps echoing in the empty library as she practically ran for the back door. But a shadow among the stacks made her jump, clutching her hand to her chest.

Adam appeared in front of her. "I have something for you."

Her heart pounded with fear. With hope. With love. "You scared me half to death!"

"That does seem to be the problem, doesn't it? I scare you, Jo, and you're not willing to overcome those fears. Well, you don't have to worry, I won't push you anymore. Here." He held up a plastic shopping bag.

"What is it?" she asked, unable to see much in the shadows.

"Your shoes. The ones you left at The Pines."

"Is that the only reason you came here tonight?" Disappointment arced through her. "Just to give me my shoes back?"

"No." He met her gaze. "I came here tonight because I missed you. Because I thought I could convince you to give us a chance. But I've been fooling myself. You've been running away from me since the morning you woke up in my bed. I guess it's time to let you go."

She took a deep breath. "That's very noble of you, Adam. But it just so happens that I'm not ready to let *you* go." Then she leaned up to kiss him, catching him by surprise.

He simply stood there for a moment, as her mouth moved over his lips. Doubt about his feelings taunted her, but it was too late to turn back now. She didn't want to turn back—not if it meant losing Adam.

But he wasn't going anywhere. When he finally realized what was happening, he locked his arms around her waist and pulled her body flush against his own. Then he kissed her hard and deep. A kiss of possession and of need. Josie matched his fire with her own, the passion building between them until it threatened to burn out of control.

When the force of their kiss propelled her against a wooden table, she lay back on it, pulling him on top of her. Books crashed to the floor as they undressed each other, clothes flying everywhere, too frantic with desire to go slowly.

Josie didn't want time to think about the ramifications ahead of them. She didn't want to think about anything except how much she loved this man.

After denying her emotions for so long, she yearned to feel. Feel the sensation of Adam's callused hands caressing her body. Feel the moist tip of his tongue on her nipples. She moaned aloud, urging him on, not holding anything back.

Her response seemed to inflame him even more. "I...can't wait," he gasped, moving his hand between her legs. "Look at me, Jo."

She opened her eyes to see him hovering over her and she instinctively knew Adam wanted her to know it was him making love to her. Wanted to banish all images of his impostor forever from her mind. He didn't know he'd done it the first night they were together.

"I love you, Adam," she whispered into the dark, cradling his cheek in her palm. "My Adam."

At the sound of his name, he thrust inside of her, joining their bodies and their souls in one long, perfect stroke. Flesh to flesh, heart to heart. She moved with him, her back sliding on the polished surface of the table. She gripped the edges to hold herself still, the climax coming upon her too fast and furious for her to ever believe this could be a mistake.

Adam caught her cries of release in his mouth, kissing her deeply as he followed her into the abyss. Later, when they could both breathe again, he wrapped his arms around her and rolled onto his back, giving her the soft pillow of his body to rest upon.

"Did I mention how stimulating I find your Thursday night book club?" he teased.

She nestled into his embrace, so relaxed she could barely move. "Next week, we're discussing *Great Expectations*. And I have a few of my own, Mr. Delaney, so I expect you to come fully prepared." Then her eyes widened in horror. "Oh, Adam, we forgot protection...."

He bent up his head to kiss her. "No, we didn't. I put on a condom."

She blinked. "You did? When?"

"Just in the nick of time," he said with a chuckle. "I guess you were too aroused to notice."

"I guess," she murmured, her afterglow swiftly fading.

He cupped her chin gently with his fingers. "Hey, what's wrong?"

"Do you always carry condoms with you?" she asked, trying to sound nonchalant. "Just in case you get lucky?"

"No," he said softly, his tone serious now. "Believe it or not, I only put this one in my wallet right before the picnic. I guess I was hoping I might get a chance to make love to you in Pleasant Valley."

She stared up at him. "But you didn't even kiss me there."

"I was going to let you make the first move," he said in his own defense. "I was *trying* to romance you."

Laughter bubbled in her throat. "Romance me? By taking me to a cave?"

"I had candles in there," he confessed. "And champagne. After I checked for snakes, I was determined to come out and entice you inside. But that's when you said you weren't feeling well and wanted to go home."

"Oh, Adam," she said with a sigh, realizing how close they'd come to losing each other. "I can't believe…"

He clamped his hand over her mouth, his eyebrows drawn down in a frown, his body tense beneath her. He laid his cheek against hers and whispered, "I think I hear something."

Josie froze, straining her ears in the silence. Then she heard something, too. The jingle of a key in the lock, followed by the sound of footsteps.

Adam's arms tightened protectively around her. "Someone's here."

"It's the janitor," she whispered, horrified that they were about to be discovered. At the very least, she'd lose her dignity, if not her job.

"We'd better get out of here," Adam said, reaching for his pants. Their clothes were scattered on the floor, some of them even hanging from books on the shelves. They dressed quickly but silently, all too aware of the janitor only a few yards away. He'd begun to whistle now, slightly off tune and moving ever closer to them.

Adam fastened his pants, then said, "We need an escape plan."

"There's a door in the back," she whispered, picking up her sandals in her hand. "But there's a good chance he'll see us if we go that way."

"Not if we cause a distraction. Are you ready to make a run for it?"

She swallowed hard, picturing herself trying to explain this incident to the head librarian. Somehow she didn't think Evelyn would believe she'd done it for research purposes. Josie shook off the image of that harrowing conversation and squared her shoulders.

"Ready."

Adam picked up one of the books that they'd pushed off the table and tossed it about twenty feet away. It landed with a loud thud on the linoleum floor. The sound made the janitor stop whistling.

"Hey," the man called out, moving in the direction of the noise, "who's there?"

"Go," Adam ordered under his breath.

Josie didn't stick around to see what happened next. She shot toward the back exit, her bare feet slapping against the hard surface of the floor. She heard Adam running right behind her as she barreled through the door.

They both kept sprinting until they reached the

safety of a tall hedge that bordered the parking lot and hid them from the view of the library.

"We made it," Josie gasped, hungry for air.

Adam's chest heaved from the exertion. When he'd caught his breath, he circled one arm protectively around her waist. "The poor guy probably thinks he met up with a ghost."

She shook her head. "Actually, he's probably calling the police. We've had vagrants try to spend the night in the library before. It hasn't happened often, but enough times to provide a plausible explanation for the noises that he heard."

"Then you're safe."

She looked up at him. "Am I?"

He pulled her closer. "Yes, Jo. You'll always be safe with me. I promise."

She leaned up to kiss him, her breasts brushing against his chest. The contact made her shiver, then she realized the reason why.

"My bra," she gasped, pulling her neckline open to stare down at her bare breasts. "I forgot my bra! It must still be in the library."

He laughed. "It's a good thing I'm around to pick up after you."

He reached behind him and pulled her lacy white bra from his back pocket. "Believe it or not, I saw it hanging from a copy of a book called *All You Could Ever Want to Know About Sex.*"

"Thank you," she said with a sigh of relief, taking

the bra from him. "I know the police probably couldn't trace it to me, but I'm not willing to take that chance."

He grinned. "Especially if they made all the librarians try it on for size, sort of like Cinderella's glass slipper."

She laughed. "And here I thought you weren't the literary type."

"Just goes to show that I have an active imagination." A wicked gleam lit his eyes. "And it's been very active lately, thanks to you."

Josie leaned up to kiss him, inhaling the musky scent of sex on his skin. "Neither one of us has to use our imaginations anymore." A siren sounded in the distance and she knew they didn't have much time. "Unless it's to come up with an alibi."

He nodded. "It sounds as if the police are on their way."

"We need to get out of here, Adam."

"Just follow me." He reached for her hand.

She took it in her own, thoroughly enjoying the adventure of falling in love. "Anywhere."

13

THE NEXT MORNING, Josie woke up in Adam's bed. The same bed where she'd first met him. Only this time she didn't recoil in horror when she saw him sleeping beside her. Instead, she moved even closer, relishing the warmth of his big, naked body against her own.

He opened his brown eyes at the contact, then smiled lazily as he hauled her closer. "Trying to seduce me again?"

"Is it working?" she asked, her hand disappearing beneath the sheet. "Ah, I can see it's working quite well."

The doorbell rang and Adam groaned in frustration as he glanced up at the clock. "It's barely past seven. Much too early for visitors. Ignore it."

"Are you sure?" she asked, her hand moving on him.

He groaned again, this time with pleasure. "I'm absolutely positive...." But the rest of his words were cut off by a quick flurry of rapid doorbell rings.

Her hand stilled on him. "Maybe it's some kind of emergency."

Adam flipped back the sheet and climbed reluctantly out of bed. "I'll bet the emergency is that Clyde Buckley ran out of beer and corn chips."

"Who is Clyde Buckley?" she asked, enjoying the view as he padded naked to his closet.

"My neighbor across the hall. A woman named Mrs. Clanahan used to live there. I liked her. She made me oatmeal cookies and adored Horatio." He pulled out a pair of blue sweatpants. "Buckley treats my place like a corner-convenience store and makes dead-cat jokes."

She smiled at his surliness. "Are you always this grouchy in the morning?"

He pulled on his sweatpants, then walked over to the bed and leaned down to kiss her. "Only when an attempt to seduce me is so rudely interrupted. Now you'll have to start all over when I come back."

"I'll be waiting right here," she promised, cuddling his pillow.

He flashed a smile, then walked out of the bedroom, closing the door firmly behind him as the doorbell rang once again.

Taking advantage of some time alone, Josie walked naked to the master bathroom. The woman she saw in the mirror above the sink couldn't stop smiling. Humming under her breath, she ran a comb through her hair, then freshened up before emerging once again.

Adam was already back in the bedroom, but instead of waiting for her in bed, he was fully dressed now and bending down to tie his sneakers.

"Are you going somewhere?" she asked, puzzled by the grim expression on his face.

He rose to his feet, then walked toward her. "Josie, it wasn't my neighbor at the door. It was the police."

"The police?" she echoed. "What did they want this early in the morning?"

"They have some questions they want me to answer about..."

Josie cut him off before he could finish. "They found out we were the ones in the library, didn't they?" She groaned inwardly, realizing she'd have some explaining to do to Evelyn Myerson after all. She moved toward the door. "Oh, Adam, let me take care of this. I'm an employee of the library and I had every right to be there."

"I can see two problems with that," he said, stepping in front of the bedroom door to block her path. "The first is that you aren't wearing any clothes." A half smile curved his mouth. "I know you're in the habit of forgetting items of clothing, but this is getting ridiculous."

A blush warmed her entire body. "I guess I wasn't thinking." Then she looked up at him. "But you mentioned two problems. What's the second one?"

"The police aren't here about our rendezvous in the library," Adam informed her. "They have a search warrant for my apartment and one of them is waiting to take me down to the station for questioning."

"Questioning about what?"

He sighed. "They're accusing me of taking pornographic pictures of underage teenage girls. They think I'm trying to peddle them to various skin magazines."

She blinked. "What?"

Adam opened the door halfway, resting one hand on the edge. "My impostor strikes again. I tried to explain that to them, but I don't think they believe me. I'm sure it will all be straightened out once we get to the station."

"Wait, Adam..."

He glanced out the door. "The cop is getting restless and you need to get ready for work." Adam turned back to her, leaning down to kiss her. "I love you, Jo. I'll be back as soon as I can."

Then he was gone. Before she even had a chance to stop him. Or tell him that she could prove he was innocent because she knew the identity of his impostor. She could hear the low drone of male voices in the living room, but couldn't make out the words.

Josie raced to the bed, picking up the clothes she'd discarded there the night before. She dressed quickly, making sure all her buttons matched and that she was wearing her bra this time.

Then she rushed to the bedroom door, almost tripping over Horatio when she opened it. The cat screeched in protest as he jumped out of her way. When she reached the living room, Adam was already gone.

A stranger wearing a dark-gray suit stood in the

center of the living room directing a crew of uniformed cops in a methodical search of the entire apartment. "You must be Ms. Sinclair."

"Yes," she replied, surprised that he knew her name. Adam must have told them she was here so they wouldn't walk in on her unexpectedly.

"I'm Detective Brent. Sorry for the intrusion, but we've got a job to do."

"Well, I can make your job a lot easier," she told him. "Because you're making a huge mistake. Adam isn't the man you want."

"Who do we want?" Detective Brent asked wryly. "His impostor?"

He was a big man, with shaggy brown hair that hung almost to his shoulders and a handlebar mustache. He looked as if he'd be more comfortable in a black leather biker's jacket than a suit.

"Yes," Josie replied evenly. "His name is Lance Golka. He posed as Adam Delaney for three months while Adam was out of the country on assignment for *Adventurer* magazine. If there are pornographic pictures being peddled using Adam's name, then Lance must be the one responsible."

The detective folded his arms across his chest. "Delaney just told us that he didn't know the identity of his impostor. That the two of you had teamed up to find him, but hadn't been successful yet."

She swallowed, knowing her story made one of them sound like a liar. Not a good image to present to the police. "I spotted my boyfriend—I mean, my *ex-*boyfriend, at an awards ceremony last week. He made me promise to keep his secret until he could come clean to Adam himself."

"I see," Detective Brent said, slowly nodding his head.

Josie couldn't tell if he believed her. She wanted to kick herself for not confiding everything about Lance to Adam last night. But that time together had been so magical between them that she hadn't wanted anything to interfere with it, content to wait until the morning.

"So this impostor passed himself off as Adam Delaney for months," Brent said. "And you're telling me that no one noticed the difference between the two of them?"

"It's not that simple," she began. "Lance impersonated Adam, but only among people who didn't know him. He was very clever that way, being careful not to reveal himself to any of Adam's friends or acquaintances who might easily point him out as a phony."

Now that Josie thought about it, she realized how very clever Lance had been. Maybe his promises to confess everything to Adam had simply been his way of buying time until his impersonation paid off. She looked up at Detective Brent and realized he looked more skeptical than ever.

"I know it seems hard to believe, but Lance knew everything about Adam's life. Down to the last detail.

So I'm sure he knew the people he had to avoid to carry it off. I can't really explain what Lance did or why he did it. I wanted to give him the benefit of the doubt, but after this..."

"Just so I'm clear," Detective Brent interjected, "this impostor was your boyfriend?"

"Yes." Josie's mind whirled as she tried to find an explanation that made sense. "But I didn't know he was impersonating Adam Delaney at the time. I thought he really was Adam Delaney. Then I met the real Adam."

"And now *he's* your boyfriend," Detective Brent deduced, his gaze straying to the open bedroom door and the visible tangled sheets.

A blush warmed her cheeks as she wondered if Adam had told him the circumstances of their first night together. She squared her shoulders. "My relationship with Adam has nothing to do with the fact that you're investigating the wrong man."

"No offense, Ms. Sinclair," Detective Brent said, "but the story both you and Delaney have told us about this so-called *impostor* doesn't really add up. If there really was an impostor, why didn't either one of you report his activities to the police before now?"

"We wanted to handle it on our own," she replied, knowing the excuse sounded lame. "To see if we could find him on our own before dragging the police into it."

"Well, we're into it now," Detective Brent said.

"Don't worry, we'll follow up on your story, Ms. Sinclair, and I'm sure we'll be contacting you with some more questions. I suggest your don't leave the jurisdiction until we get this matter all settled."

She stared at him, knowing full well that he didn't believe her or Adam. In fact, he was insinuating that she might be involved in the crime as well!

Knowing it would be futile to stay and argue with him, she headed toward the front door. Horatio peeked around the corner of the kitchen, obviously upset at this invasion into his domain. Josie was upset, too, but more angry at herself than the police. It was her fault Adam was under investigation. If she had exposed Lance when she'd seen him at the awards ceremony over a week ago, none of this would be happening.

Now she just had to find a way to stop it.

THREE HOURS LATER, Adam arrived at the library. He'd spent two of those hours trying to convince the police that his impostor was to blame for those pornographic pictures. When they had started postulating that Josie might be in on the crime, he'd known it was time to call in reinforcements.

So he'd placed a call to his private investigator, Cole Rafferty, asking him to come down to the station and verify his story. Rafferty was a former cop, which gave him more clout with the police than a regular civilian. When Rafferty told them that Adam had hired him weeks ago to investigate the activities of a man who had been impersonating him, the cops let him go.

That was when he discovered the only evidence they had against him was an envelope full of risqué pictures of scantily clad teenage girls. Pictures with fingerprints on them that didn't belong to him.

Now he was here to tell Josie the charges pending against him had been dropped. But when he walked inside the library, her desk was empty.

"May I help you?" asked a voice behind him.

He turned to see a middle-aged woman with platinum hair and placid hazel eyes. She wore a conservative gray suit, much like Josephine had worn when he'd seen her at the library the first time. "I'm looking for Josie."

Her mouth pinched. "You must be Mr. Delaney."

"That's right." Her reaction made him wonder if the police had already been there. "I need to speak with her as soon as possible."

"I'm sorry, Mr. Delaney, but Josie isn't here."

He glanced at his watch, a little disoriented by everything that had happened since he'd woken up this morning. "Wasn't she scheduled to work today?"

"Yes, but she called in sick." The woman's face softened a little. "Actually, I'm quite worried about her. She didn't sound well at all on the telephone."

His gut tightened. Josie couldn't possibly believe those accusations against him, could she? He banished the question as soon as it entered his mind. If there was one quality he admired about her, it was her loyalty.

"Don't worry," he assured the woman, turning toward the door. "I'll make sure she's all right."

Ten minutes later, he pulled up in front of her town house, parking behind a white SUV that had seen better days.

Climbing out of his Camaro, he was surprised to see the door to her town house standing wide open. And even more surprised to see a man standing just inside the foyer talking to Josie.

That man was Lance Golka.

Adam started up the walk, wondering what in the world Lance was doing here. Then he got his answer when he saw his old college roommate put his arms around her. He stopped cold, the world shifting beneath his feet as the awful truth finally hit him.

Adam had found his impostor.

"PLEASE, JOSIE," LANCE PLEADED, "just give me one more chance. I know we can make it work this time."

Her former boyfriend had just enveloped her in a ferocious bear hug, his grip so tight she could barely breathe. After leaving Adam's apartment, she called Lance using the cell phone number he'd given her when he'd visited the library the Wednesday before.

She'd asked him to come to her place as soon as possible. Her plan had been to convince him to turn himself over to the police. To her surprise, he'd agreed without much argument, even asking her to drive him to the station.

Now it appeared he was having second thoughts.

"I know I screwed up," he continued, "but we can start over again. Just you and me. We'll get in my SUV and just keep on driving until all our problems are behind us. I love you, Josie Sinclair. You know I love you."

Enough was enough. She broke out of his embrace just in time to see Adam standing on her front porch.

"What the hell is going on here?" Adam demanded and looked between the two of them, his jaw clenched. "No, don't tell me. I think I can guess."

Lance moved protectively in front of her. "I'm sorry you had to find out this way, Delaney. Josie and I didn't want to hurt you."

"Adam, it's not what you think," Josie explained, stepping around Lance.

"You mean Lance isn't my impostor?"

She swallowed, devastated by the raw pain she saw on his face. She couldn't lie to him anymore. "Yes, he is."

"And you've known that from the beginning," he accused. "Stringing me along while you pretended to hate every minute of it." His face grew red with fury. "Was climbing into my bed that first night part of the plan, too?"

"That's enough," Lance snapped. "None of this is Josie's fault. The only thing you can blame her for is caring about me too much. I'm to blame for all the rest."

Adam took a step forward, his fists clenched at his sides. "Oh, I do blame you, Golka. What the hell have you been doing in my life?"

"Just getting a taste of what should have been mine," Lance replied, not sounding the least bit contrite. "You won the photo contest that I wanted to enter. You got the job that I had dreamed about forever. Everything fell into place in your life, Adam, thanks to that contest. Thanks to me. I figured you owed me."

Josie stared at her ex-boyfriend, aware that he was revealing a side she'd never seen before. A sniveling, selfish side. One that made her realize she'd been a fool for keeping his secret.

"Like hell," Adam growled, refusing even to look at her.

That hurt her almost as much as his anger. He wouldn't acknowledge her in any way. All his attention was focused on Lance.

"You stole part of my life and almost ruined me in the process," Adam exclaimed. "I don't owe you a damn thing."

Josie closed her eyes, wondering if this could possibly get any worse. She didn't have to wonder long.

"And you stole my girlfriend," Lance retorted, tipping his chin in the air. "For a little while anyway. So I'd say we're more than even. You can have your life back. All I want is Josie."

"Fine." His jaw clenched. "You can have her." Then Adam turned around and strode down the steps.

"Wait," she cried, starting after him.

Lance grabbed her arm. "Let him go, Josie. Adam Delaney's not the right man for you. He's not even willing to stay and fight for you."

She wrenched out of his grasp, but by the time she reached the curb, Adam was already peeling away in his Camaro. She stood in the empty street, watching the sports car speed away until she couldn't see it anymore.

Lance walked up beside her. "I meant what I said before, Josie. I want us to start over. A clean state. No more lies. No more Adam. I think we could make it work."

She slowly turned to face him, envisioning what a life with Lance would have been like. They would have always played it safe, exchanging pragmatism for passion. Security instead of spontaneity. The man standing in front of her wasn't even thirty years old yet and his life was already full of regrets.

Josie could only be thankful she hadn't played it safe. Adam had packed more joy and pain and adventure and danger into a few short weeks than she'd experienced in a lifetime. Even now, she couldn't be sorry.

Lance took her hand, mistaking her silence for consideration of his proposal. "Say you'll be my wife. Marry me, Josie."

Those three little words would have pleased her once. A passionless marriage might be safe, but it was also empty. Lonely. A life with Adam offered no guarantees, but she knew now that the worst disaster that could befall her would be living her life without passion in it.

"I can't marry you, Lance."

His face fell. "You love him."

"Yes."

"So Adam wins again." He dropped her hand, his expression growing cold. "He wins my woman, just like he won my career and my life."

She wanted to shake him out of his endless cycle of self-pity and make him see the truth. "How could I be yours, Lance, when I didn't even know who you really were? I'm not sure *you* even know who you really are. Stop trying to live Adam's life and start living your own."

He took a deep breath, shaking his head. "You make it sound so simple."

"It's not simple," she told him. "It's hard and scary and uncertain. That's what makes it exciting. If you want to be a photographer, then just do it. But with your own name and your own talent." Then she shivered, thinking of another requirement. "And with models over the age of eighteen."

"Those girls *told* me they were legal age," Lance replied in his own defense. "They even signed release forms to that effect."

"Then show those to the police and you'll probably get off without any charges."

"Right. Adam will want to lock me up and throw away the key. I've never seen him so angry."

Neither had she. But more than that, she'd seen pain. Raw pain that had glittered like shards of amber glass in his eyes. She'd been so concerned about getting hurt, Josie hadn't realized how much she could hurt him. "So what are you going to do?"

Lance thought about it for a moment, then looked at Josie. "If I go to the police, will you come with me?"

She wanted to cry out in frustration, impatient to get to Adam. "I really think you should do this on your own."

He met her gaze. "Just help me take this first step. Otherwise I might chicken out. I'm tired of running away, Josie. But I'm just not used to the alternative."

She couldn't turn him down, not when she saw so much of herself in him. Josephine Sinclair had been scared of life, too, until Adam Delaney had come crashing into it. And despite everything, she had Lance to thank for it. Without him, she and Adam never would have met.

"All right," she agreed at last. "I'll take my car and follow you down to the police station."

"What should I do after I deal with the police? I mean, assuming they let me off without pressing any charges."

"That's up to you," she said, climbing up the porch

steps to retrieve her purse from the house. Josie still couldn't get the stark expression on Adam's face out of her mind. Her betrayal had hurt him deeply and she hoped he could forgive her.

"I guess so," Lance said, his voice full of wonder at all the possibilities. "I've spent so many years wishing I was Adam Delaney that I'm not sure who I am anymore. Maybe it's time I found out."

"I have faith in you, Lance," Josie said, trying to stay strong. "That's all you need. Faith, and maybe a little bit of luck."

"I know." Lance pulled his car keys out of his pocket. "I guess I should wish good luck to you, too, Josie." He shrugged resignedly. "With Adam, I mean."

"Thanks." She was definitely going to need it.

14

JOSIE WAS ALMOST FRANTIC by the time she finally reached the door to Adam's apartment. Several hours had passed since he'd roared away from her town house in his Camaro. Unfortunately, Lance's confession at the police station had taken longer than she'd expected. The end result being that none of the girls or their parents would press charges if he agreed to turn over all the photographs, negatives and undeveloped rolls of film.

Lance had eagerly agreed, though he'd been surprised Adam hadn't filed charges against him yet. Josie was surprised, too, wondering if Adam was just biding his time or if he had a more fitting revenge in mind. But Josie didn't care about that at the moment. All she wanted was to see Adam's face. To make him listen to her until he understood that she loved him and had never meant to hurt him.

After taking a moment to straighten her clothes and clear her throat, Josie reached out and rang the doorbell. Maybe Adam had calmed down by now and realized that she could never choose Lance over him. But those hopes faded when Adam didn't answer the door. She rang the bell again, determined not to leave until he gave her a chance to explain.

"He's gone," a rough voice said behind her.

She turned to see a man standing in the hallway, the door to his apartment half open. He was pushing sixty, with a bad comb-over and a generic beer in his hand. The T-shirt he wore stretched over his pot belly. She knew from Adam's description of the man that he could only be Clyde Buckley.

"Gone?" she echoed. "You mean Adam?"

"That's right. He left about a couple of hours ago. Packed his bags and just took off."

She stared at him, not wanting to believe it could be true. "Where did he go?"

The older man shrugged. "Can't remember exactly what he told me. Niagara Falls, maybe. Or Nairobi. Something that starts with an N."

That narrowed it down. "You're sure about this?"

"Why would I lie?" Buckley scowled at her. "I'm a trustworthy guy, even if Delaney refused my offer to take care of his damn cat. He actually took the damn thing with him."

This news gave her some hope. Surely Adam wouldn't drag Horatio halfway around the world with him.

"He said he had a friend that would watch out for the fleabag." Buckley smothered a belch before taking another long sip of his beer.

"Is that all he said?" she asked, desperate for details. Who was this friend? And where was Adam going?

"Hell if I know," Buckley replied with a shrug. "Delaney muttered something about running out of people to trust. Let me tell you, the guy sure wasn't acting very neighborly."

She slumped against the wall, knowing she'd brought this all on herself. Adam was still furious with her. Worse, he was running away. He could be on his way to anywhere in the world by now and all she knew was that his destination started with an N. She supposed she could try at the magazine but they likely had a policy against giving out personal information like that.

Which meant she'd have to wait until he returned from his trip. The delay rankled her, but at least it would give her time to come up with an explanation for keeping Lance's secret that didn't sound as utterly foolish as the truth.

"You got any aspirin on you?" Buckley asked, rubbing his temple. "I've got a hell of a headache."

"No, I don't," she replied, mentally adding up all the vacation time she'd accumulated at the library. Once Adam came back, she'd want to spend every extra moment with him to make up for the time they'd lost.

"Delaney always had aspirin," Buckley grumbled, moving back inside his apartment. "I just hope the new guy who moves in isn't stingy."

"New guy?" Josie followed him, planting her hand against his apartment door to keep him from closing it. "What are you talking about?"

"The new tenant. Delaney ain't coming back."

Josie stumbled back and the door closed in her face. She stood alone in the hallway, trying to absorb that he was really gone. After a few moments, her shock turned to frustration. How dare Adam give up on them so easily! She loved him and she wasn't about to let him do the running away this time.

No matter what it took.

THREE DAYS LATER, Josie sat in the Denver International Airport reviewing the checklist in her hand. A voice sounded over the loudspeaker, making her pause in her perusal.

"First call for Flight Number 118 to New York, Paris and New Zealand, now boarding. First call for Flight 118."

That was her plane. Anticipation welled up inside of her as she stood up and prepared to board. The concourse was crowded for a Monday, though she'd skipped the long lines at the lunch counters, too anxious to eat.

She'd spent the entire weekend preparing for this trip, but had she thought of everything? Her gaze fell to the list in her hand once more and she quickly scanned it to make certain she hadn't forgotten anything.

1. Locate Adam.

Josie had tracked down Shondra on Friday evening at the Alligator Bar where she moonlighted as a bartender on the weekends. At first, Shondra had been reluctant to reveal Adam's whereabouts, but Josie had finally convinced her that she wasn't going to back off. Before she left the bar, she'd acquired a taste for straight talk and Irish iced tea that had earned Shondra's grudging respect.

That was the easy part. The hard part had been convincing herself that she could handle the wilds of the west coast of New Zealand. Adam was on an extensive photo shoot somewhere near the remote town of Harihari. It would take her three days to get there, with layovers in Los Angeles and Melbourne, Australia, before she finally reached Queenstown, New Zealand. From there she'd have to take a helicopter to fly her to wherever Adam was staying. Preparing for the trip had led her to the next item on her list:

2. *Research New Zealand.*

Saturday had been spent on the Internet and at the library, where she'd researched every aspect of her upcoming trip. Josie had learned that New Zealand in July had a mild climate, so she'd packed accordingly. She'd also discovered more than she ever wanted to know about some of the native plants and animals. There weren't any venomous snakes to worry about, but plenty of mosquitoes and sand flies.

Her gaze moved to the next item on the list:

3. *Clean out bank accounts.*

The cost of the round-trip plane ticket alone had almost maxed out her lone credit card. Which meant she'd have to spend most of her savings on hotels, food, transportation in New Zealand and other necessities. If she ran out of money on the trip, she'd just have to figure out some way to get by.

"Second call to board Flight 118 to New Zealand. Second call to board Flight 118 to New Zealand."

Josie quickly scanned the rest of the list, mentally checking off the other items. It seemed as if she'd prepared for everything—except the possibility that Adam might reject her. But she'd have plenty of time to worry about that on the plane. Picking up her carry-on bag from the floor, she turned toward the boarding gate.

"Josie!"

She glanced over her shoulder and saw Evelyn Myerson running toward her. The head librarian had tried to talk Josie out of this trip, even as she agreed to give her the time off.

"I'm so glad I caught you," Evelyn said, gasping for breath.

"What is it?" Josie asked, concerned by the pale expression on the woman's face. "What's wrong?"

"There was a call for you at the library. Some woman named Shondra from that magazine."

Hope flared within her. Had Adam come back? "Shondra O'Conner? What did she say? Is it about Adam?"

"Yes," Evelyn said, taking a step closer to her and placing a comforting hand on her shoulder. "You'd better sit down."

Hope fizzled as the fear of apprehension paralyzed her. "Tell me."

"He's missing."

"Missing," Josie whispered, reminding herself to breathe. Missing wasn't good, not good at all, but there were worse alternatives.

"Apparently, he went out for a photo shoot yesterday in the bush without taking a wilderness guide along with him." She took a deep breath. "He never came back."

"That doesn't mean something happened to him," Josie said, trying to convince herself as much as Evelyn. "Maybe he just wanted to strike out on his own."

"Maybe," Evelyn agreed, but sounded skeptical. "The point is that you can't go on this trip now. Not when you don't know what you're getting into there. I think it would be much better for you to stay here and wait for news. And Shondra agrees with me."

There was no question in Josie's mind. "I can't stay here. Adam might need me."

Evelyn shook her head. "You can't do him any good if you get lost, too. Face the facts, Josie. You've got absolutely no experience in surviving in the wilderness. You'd be completely out of your element. Who knows what dangers might await you there?"

Josie knew Evelyn was right. Her research had told

her that much. Just like she knew that *reading* about fording a river was very different from actually *doing* it. Her experience was limited to what she'd read in guidebooks. How far would that get her?

A buzz sounded over the loudspeaker, followed by a voice that said, *"Final boarding call for Flight 118 to New Zealand."*

It was now or never. Josie had a decision to make—one that could literally be life or death.

"Final boarding call for Flight 118 to New Zealand."

ADAM HAD SPENT A WEEK alone, battling the elements and the rugged terrain on the west coast of New Zealand and he still couldn't get Josephine Sinclair out of his mind. He'd escaped the watchful eye of his guide a few days ago, who had acted more like a nanny than a wilderness expert. He'd been camping out on the bank of the Whataroa River ever since, telling himself he was having a great time.

But he'd never been a good liar.

Unlike Josie. He still couldn't believe she'd betrayed him that way, especially after the way they'd made love at the library. The passion he'd seen in her eyes wasn't a lie. Neither was her desire for him. Adam knew enough about women to be sure of that.

Which left him even more confused about her deception. Adam stood on an outcropping of high rock overlooking the river, debating the right angle for his next shot. From his vantage point, it looked as if he wouldn't have to go far for the pictures he wanted to take today.

Reaching into his knapsack, Adam strapped on a bright-orange harness vest, affixing it to his upper torso with hooks and Velcro. A long, double-strength nylon tether hung from the vest. He looped the end of it around the small trunk of a tree overhanging the rock, checking the stability of it before he put it to the full test.

His motion limited now, Adam picked up his camera, making a quick check to be sure he had enough film and battery power left to get him through the shoot. Once he was up in the air, he didn't want to come down again until he was done.

He'd obtained some great pictures in the last week and couldn't wait to develop them. This would be the best one yet—another guaranteed nominee for the Insanity Award. But in his mind, it still wasn't good enough. The perfect shot remained elusively out of his reach.

After tugging on the harness strap to make certain once again that it was secure, he grabbed his camera and hung it over his neck. Then he carefully stepped to the edge of the rock. A waterfall tumbled only twenty feet below, offering a breathtaking view of nature at its most primitive. A cool mist of water dampened his face, causing him to put the lens cap on the camera until he was ready for the shot. The camera was made to withstand the elements and had been priced accordingly, but he didn't want to take any unnecessary chances.

Adam inched closer to the edge, raising his camera and adjusting the lens. His thoughts drifted to Josie again and he wondered if she was working at the library now. No, more likely asleep in her bed, given the time change.

Or asleep in Lance's bed.

He slipped on the slick, mossy surface of the rock, almost losing his balance. Scrambling to retain his footing, he reached for an overhanging tree branch—and missed. The next thing he knew, Adam found himself suspended in midair, swinging back and forth in his harness, which was the only thing keeping him from tumbling into the treacherous falls.

"Great," Adam muttered, trying to rationally assess his situation. It didn't look good. He tried to lengthen his swinging motion as he hung in the harness, pumping his legs like he'd done as a kid on the school swing set. Only the harness strap was too short for him to gain enough momentum to reach the rock. He tried to pull himself up on the cord, hand over hand, but it was too thin and slippery to get a good grip.

So he hung there, suspended in air and wondering if the Insanity Award would be presented to him posthumously next year. After a while, Adam's mouth hitched up in a smile at the irony of it all. He'd lost his concentration thinking about Josie. Taking risks in his career was an everyday occurrence, but the first sign of risking his heart had made him turn tail and run. And this incident just proved that he couldn't run away from Josie. She was in his heart and his mind twenty-four hours a day. Adam loved her. He'd never stopped loving her.

Only it was too late to tell her that now. He deserved an award all right—the Chicken Award for not having the courage to stay in Denver and fight for the woman he loved.

As the day wore on, Adam hung suspended from the tree branch, wondering how long he could survive there without food or water. He hadn't seen a soul for the last three days, so he knew his chances of someone rescuing him were slim. Fatigue overtook him in mid-afternoon and he found himself dozing off and on, dreams of Josie flitting through the haze of semiconsciousness.

"Adam, are you all right?"

He opened his eyes and saw her standing on the edge of the rock. Then he closed them again, not wanting to wake up and lose this image of Josie, so clear and vivid in his mind.

"Adam!"

He thought he smelled jasmine. Then something hit him in the gut and he opened his eyes again. The Josie in his dreams was throwing dirt clods at him. One hit him in the knee, followed by an extra-large clod that careered off his elbow, the impact bringing him fully to his senses.

"Ow, that hurt," he said, reaching up to rub his elbow. Then he squinted at her. "Josie?"

Maybe he was hallucinating. It was a balmy day, not more than seventy degrees, but he had been hanging in the sun for several hours. Josie couldn't be in New Zealand, much less standing on the bank of the Whataroa River.

"Are you all right, Adam?" she asked, concern pooling in her green eyes. A khaki backpack was slung over her shoulders and tiny scratches covered her legs and arms. She wore thick hiking boots and a khaki hat concealed most of her blond hair.

"My elbow's a little sore, but otherwise, I'm fine." The possibility that she wasn't an illusion was slowly seeping into his brain. "I'm just a little hung up right now."

"This isn't funny," she scolded. "I can't believe you'd do something like this just for a silly picture! From now on, you are not allowed to take these kind of crazy chances with your life."

"Says who?" he challenged, never so happy to be lectured in his life.

"Me," she replied stubbornly, folding her arms across her chest. "You definitely need someone to take care of you. I've got sunscreen in my bag, along with some industrial-strength mosquito repellent and bandages. I brought extra bottles of water. Some vitamins and aspirin..."

As Josie recited her long list of safety precautions,

he realized she'd never looked more beautiful to him. Even with the peeling sunburn on her red nose and the tangled strands of limp blond hair dangling from underneath her hat.

"How did you find me?" he asked, finally interrupting her litany of medical supplies.

"Your guide picked up your trail two days after you dumped him," she replied, waving away a sand fly. "The poor man's been hiking back and forth between here and the main camp every evening to check on you. Apparently, you were such a miserable client he was as happy to get rid of you as you were to get rid of him. Of course, he didn't know you'd gotten yourself in *this* predicament."

"That explains how you found me, but it doesn't explain why you're here."

Her face softened. "I'm here because I love you, Adam. I'll follow you everywhere if I have to, just to keep you safe."

Her words made him feel almost giddy, but there was still something he needed to know. "What about Lance?"

She took a step closer to him. "I first saw Lance at the awards ceremony, where he asked me to let him be the one to tell you he was the impostor. I thought I could trust him, but I should have known better."

"So you're not in love with him?"

"There's only one man I love." She smiled. "One man who can make me angry and crazy and deliriously happy all in one day. One man who can make me ache for his touch. It's you, Adam. Only you. And that's something I intend to keep telling you until you believe it. Even if it means I have to follow you up the Himalayas or down the Nile or across the Sahara Desert on a camel."

"Will you follow me to Okariko?" he asked softly, aching to hold her. "It's about twenty miles south of here."

Tears of relief and joy shimmered in her eyes. "I'll follow you anywhere, Adam. Whether it's twenty miles or twenty-thousand miles. But why do you want to go to Okariko?"

He grinned. "Because I think it would make a great place for a honeymoon."

Her smile widened. "Oh, Adam. I love you so much."

"Then get me down from here, so you can show me."

She picked up a coil of rope he'd left on the ground and tossed one end to him. He snatched it out of the air, then pulled himself, hand over hand, to where she stood on the rock. When his feet reached solid ground, Josie pulled him into the safety of her arms.

"Now I've got you just where I want you." She leaned up to kiss him.

"Wait," he said, stepping away from her. He pulled the camera over his head, then set the timer before carefully placing it on a rocky ledge in front of them.

Adam hurried back to her side, hastily brushing the soil from his wrinkled clothes and rubbing ruefully at the three-day-old growth of whiskers on his jaw.

Josie looked up at him, her face streaked with dirt and perspiration, the wrinkled khaki hat pulled down almost to her eyebrows.

Adam wrapped himself around her, pulling her close as he gazed into her eyes. "After all these years, I've finally achieved what I've been searching for my entire career. What's driven me to the peaks of mile-high mountains and depths of bottomless gorges all over the world."

"What is it?" she asked, curiosity shining in her emerald eyes.

"The perfect shot," he replied, as the camera flashed a picture of the two of them holding each other. A picture that would last forever—just like their love.

* * *

*Don't forget we have a new story from
Kristin Gabriel in the summer.*

EVER AFTER
by Fiona Hood-Stewart

"An enthralling page turner—
not to be missed." —*New York Times*
bestselling author Joan Johnston

**She belongs to a world of wealth,
politics and social climbing. But
now Elm must break away to find
happily ever after...**

Elm MacBride can no longer sit back and
watch her corrupt and deceitful husband's
ascent to power and his final betrayal sends her
fleeing to Switzerland where she meets
Irishman Johnny Graney. When her husband's
actions threaten to destroy her, Johnny must
save not only their love but Elm's life...

ISBN 07783 2078 2

Published 15th April 2005

SILHOUETTE®

Desire 2 in 1

is proud to introduce

DYNASTIES:
THE DANFORTHS

Meet the Danforths—a family of prominence...
tested by scandal, sustained by passion!

Coming Soon!
Twelve thrilling stories in six 2-in-1 volumes: